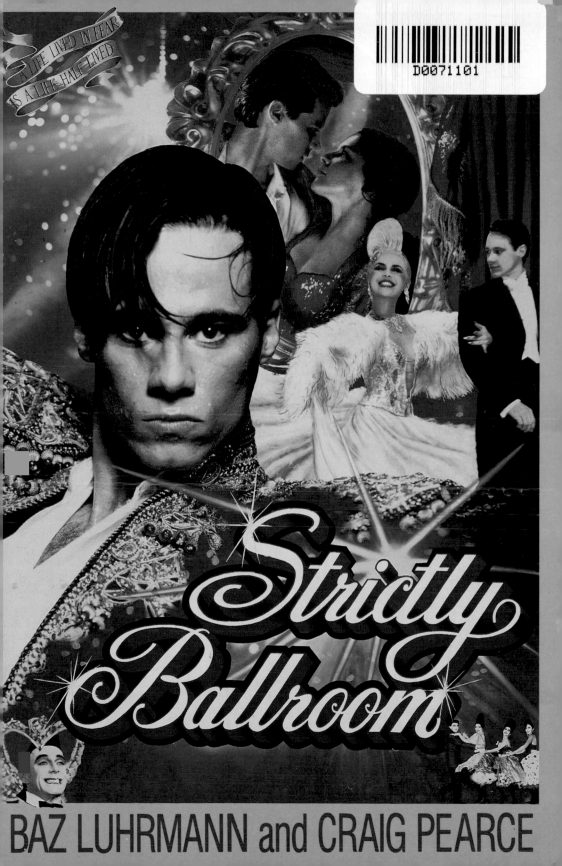

A LIFE LIVED IN FEAR IS A LIFE HALF LIVED

D0071101

Strictly Ballroom

BAZ LUHRMANN and CRAIG PEARCE

BAZ LUHRMANN's background is broadly based in the performing arts. He was an actor in *Winter of Our Dreams* and co-director and performer in the docu-drama *Kids of the Cross*. In 1986, while a student at the National Institute of Dramatic Art he devised the first stage version of *Strictly Ballroom* with other students and directed the production. At the World Youth Theatre Festival in Czechoslovakia he received the Best Director award. In 1987 he co-wrote and directed *Lake Lost* for the Australian Opera. On graduating from NIDA he was appointed Artistic Director of the Six Years Old Company and revived *Strictly Ballroom* for a successful season at the Wharf Theatre in Sydney and World Expo in Brisbane. Baz and his team produced the Coca Cola Bottler's Dance Hall as part of the 1989 Festival of Sydney. In 1990 he directed *La Boheme* for the Australian Opera and will direct *Midsummer Night's Dream* in 1993.

CRAIG PEARCE is also a NIDA graduate. Craig played Gary in *Strictly Ballroom* (the play) with the Six Years Old Company, Sasho in *Say Goodbye to the Past*, Griffin Theatre Company, Laertes in *Hamlet*, Phillip St Theatre and Balthasar in the Sydney Theatre Company's *Romeo and Juliet*. Television credits include *E Street*, *Rafferty's Rules*, *Vietnam*, *The Miraculous Mellops* and *Night Noises*. Film credits include a documentary for the National Heart Foundation and *The Big Gig*, *Vicious* and *Mad Bomber in Love*. In addition Craig directed the documentary *Brat Cats*.

Strictly Ballroom won the Prix de la Jeunesse for Best Film and was runner up in the Camera d'Or prize section at the 1992 Cannes Film Festival, Best Film of the Festival – Audience Vote, at the Sydney, Melbourne and Toronto Film Festivals, and was nominated for 13 AFI awards.

Strictly Ballroom

BAZ LUHRMANN AND CRAIG PEARCE

from a screenplay by

BAZ LUHRMANN AND ANDREW BOVELL

CURRENCY PRESS • SYDNEY

First published in 1992 by
Currency Press Ltd
PO Box 452, Paddington NSW 2021, Australia

National Library of Australia
Cataloguing-in-Publication data

    Luhrmann, Baz.
      Strictly ballroom.

      ISBN 0 86819 359 3

      1. Strictly ballroom (Motion picture). 2. Ballroom dancing –
      Competitions – Australia – Drama. 3. Dancers – Australia – Drama.
      4. Motion picture plays. I. Pearce, Craig. II. Strictly ballroom
      (Motion picture). III.Title.

    791.4372

Printed by Griffin Press, Adelaide
Cover design by Trevor Hood
Stills photography by Philip Le Masurier
Publisher's note: this is the reading script and includes only those
camera directions which are essential to the story.

Contents

This screenplay is dedicated to

Ted Albert

and

Pat Thomson

From the Producer

Tristram Miall

At the end of 1988 Ted Albert and I approached Baz Luhrmann about turning the fifty minute stage production of *Strictly Ballroom* into a feature film almost double that length. We knew that the play had worked in front of a wide variety of audiences in Sydney, Brisbane and Czechoslovakia where it had won awards for best play and best direction at an international drama festival in Bratislava.

We also knew it had the three key elements we were looking for – humour, music and dance. Ted loved the old Hollywood MGM musicals of the thirties and forties. What we wanted to create was an all-Australian contemporary realisation of that tradition. It was a bold idea given that dance movies barely feature at all in Australian feature production. At Baz's insistence and with our full support, boldness and a refusal to compromise became the standard for the film.

The development of the script was a fascinating, frustrating and finally fulfilling journey, which took us all down many dead-ends over a two year period. Those dead-ends featured allegorical sub-plots, that we later realised added confusion, interrupted the energy and cost too much to shoot. What better reasons could there be for dropping them? The strength of the script came from its simplicity. The challenge was always to get the structure right.

An early trip to Cannes to excite overseas distributors with our script was unsuccessful. Why couldn't they see what we could see so clearly? Baz acted out scenes in front of jaded Hollywood distributors, waltzing one minute, doing a rumba the next. Despite this, none wanted to bite. We did our best to give a taste of the style of the film and particularly the humour – without success – 'Strictly What? did you say, Strictly Boring?'

Getting any feature film up and made is a roller-coaster ride, with exhilarating highs and gut-wrenching lows. The worst came just as the script had reached a stage where we were all happy with it. My partner Ted Albert, the one of us who had seen the original play and suggested it as our first feature, died suddenly of a heart attack.

In the end, with help first and foremost from Ted's widow, Popsy Albert who joined the film as Executive Producer; but also from Andrew Pike at Ronin Films, and the Australian Film Finance Corporation and many good friends, perseverance won out and we moved into production. That was another exhilarating journey. This script is the result of the strong and sustained belief of the key people involved in its creation. The film that grew out of it reflects the passion of all of those who then contributed to its realisation.

Sydney, 1992

More Than Just Song and Dance

Peter Crayford

Australia comes of age in *Strictly Ballroom*. It is something
more than a pastiche of Hollywood dance films of the forties
and more than just the struggle of two young people to
crash through the restrictions of an authoritarian Dance
Federation to express themselves.

A film about growing up, it tells us something, not just
about its two dancing protagonists but about ourselves, of
where we have come as a country over the past three
decades.

Three competing worlds collide in this exuberant musical
comedy. They broadly define the type of community in
which we live and help give definition to the kind of
community which we are becoming.

There is the broadly acted world of the Dance Federation,
almost cartoon-like in its bravado and gaudiness and
exemplified by the tyrannical Barry Fife (Bill Hunter). He's a
throwback to the fifties: to an Australia which had a closed
mind, atrophied with the values of a bludgeoning Anglo-
Irish authoritarianism.

Barry is the president of the Dance Federation but he
could be the president of a moribund RSL. For him rules
weren't made to be broken; to do so would threaten the
flimsy power of his fiefdom and his crowning glory, the Pan-
Pacific Grand Prix Dance Competition.

The world which proffers the most threat to Barry's is
one he has never seen. Its values are adopted by the two

main protagonists Scott (Paul Mercurio) and Fran (Tara Morice). Scott is from a well known dancing family and is expected to win the Pan Pacific Finals with his regular partner Liz (Gia Carides). But he teams up with the inexperienced Fran and it is from her Spanish immigrant family that he learns what dancing, and by implication life, is all about.

There is a marvellous night scene which takes place at the rear of Fran's shop-cum-home when Scott is invited to dance the pasa doble. He dances it in the style that his parents and the Federation have taught him. But it has no heart, no soul and is kitsch. Fran's very Spanish grandmother and father show them the real pasa doble, doing the flamenco on the back veranda crashing their heels and affecting the role of the bull and the matador. It's a most spine-tingling exhibition and affectingly danced by Antonio Vargas and Armonia Benedito.

This scene is, in its own small way, an affirmation of multicultural Australia and shows what immigrant people can contribute. Here they are intangible values but ones which can be recognised by us all as the audience response at the Pan Pacific Finals, where Scott and Fran perform, makes abundantly clear.

The third world in collision belongs to Scott's hapless parents, Doug and Shirley Hastings played by Barry Otto and Pat Thomson. They have nurtured their boy to be the success they never were. Oppressed by the Federation's rules which robbed them of their creativity, they live on repressed memories of a glory they were denied. When their story is finally presented it is ingeniously expressionistic and very funny. Yet it shows the damage which Barry Fife's hypocritical values have had on their personal lives and on the nation.

Strictly Ballroom recognises almost subliminal psychological and political change in Australian identity and expresses it as a clash of cinematic styles as well as of characters and values. It will be seen as important a film, in defining ourselves to ourselves and to others, as *Crocodile*

Dundee was in the eighties.

It is inventive, entertaining and uplifting. From the moment the curtains part and the sparkle passes over the titles Baz Luhrmann's direction displays the confidence and the irony to bring off a remarkable film.

The performances are uneven: Paul Mercurio is convincing but a better dancer than actor. Tara Morice shows great promise in her role as Fran, who begins as an ingenue and blossoms into a woman. While many of the smaller parts played by Gia Carides, Bill Hunter, Barry Otto and Pat Thomson are comic book inspired, those of Antonio Vargas and Armonia Benedito are almost 'neo-realistic'.

This clash of styles gives the film much of its inventiveness. The polished editing makes the film seem much shorter than it is, giving it great momentum. *Strictly Ballroom* has zip, humour and emotion and deserves the success it is destined for.

Financial Review, 21 August, 1992

Waltzing out of the Outback into the Ballroom

Deborah Jones

You could scarcely find three more superficially different films but if *Strictly Ballroom* has a place in our history it is as successor to *The Man from Snowy River* and *Crocodile Dundee*.

Those two films, made in 1982 and 1986 and coincidentally our most popular films in box office terms to date, each tell a good yarn likely to appeal to a wide range of people, but there's more. There's an underlying sense that something is understood about the fact of being Australian.

The Man from Snowy River told us we had a past to be proud of and to be celebrated. It was the myth of the wide, brown land and the hard-working farmer, shared by so few of us but recognised as being truly Australian.

By 1986 we were ready to acknowledge our essentially urban character, but filtered through the Outback spirit, which we weren't quite ready to relinquish. Mick Dundee was our man, equally at home in Kakadu or Queens.

In 1992, the world is a suburb, but not only that. The suburb is also a world. In *Strictly Ballroom*, there is an embracing of all the people who are us.

It is a film about family fights and lost opportunities, about a rebellious son and a disappointed father, a frustrated mother and a young woman trying to find her place in the world. And, miraculously, this film is a comedy.

With flashes of light from a sequinned jacket, *Strictly Ballroom* lightly illuminates a world that embraces young and old, male and female, migrant and home-grown, powerful and powerless, beautiful and plain.

Scott Hastings (Paul Mercurio) might be a pure Aussie lad, but he ends up with Spanish Fran (Tara Morice), whose extended family isn't there to provide comic relief but is in fact treated with greater respect than any other and provides an insight into what families might ideally be like.

So *Strictly Ballroom* is both *for* the family, in that it eschews sex and violence, and *about* the family as a social unit at a time when family values are being widely discussed.

Strictly Ballroom celebrates the small victories of the ordinary people, and, moreover, says they are possible. It is a powerful message to a country with a strong smell of defeat in its nostrils.

There is even, in the flamboyant, larger-than-life setting of the film, a nod to the spirit and creativity of the gay community.

All this, presented with a strong dash of Aussie humour that owes much to the wit of Barry Humphries.

But why should the film 'travel' well? Why, as the *Strictly Ballroom* international steamroller moves into full gear, will fifty other countries be seeing the film between now and Christmas?

Perhaps the answer is that to be Australian now is to be much more like other people, anywhere, than we may have admitted in the past.

Australian, 1992

Film's Success is Strictly Wonderful

The success of the film *Strictly Ballroom*, is heartening at a time when the economy and the film industry seem to be in the doldrums. To be one of only two films shown at the Special Midnight Screening of the 45th International Cannes Film Festival was a notable achievement for a thoroughly Australian production and the naturalness of its star, Paul Mercurio, was as affecting as the film itself.

Funding bodies were largely unsympathetic when the film was mooted over two years ago. Its lack of an international star was thought a disadvantage. Yet it developed its own camaraderie, largely due to the directorship of Baz Luhrmann, and a fierce loyalty to him ensured its success. Costing a mere $3.5 million, this production shows ingenuity, tenacity and hard work can overcome the most daunting artistic obstacles. Its appeal depends upon some subtle human factors of which large budgets are no guarantee.

Strictly Ballroom reveals something of the nature of Australia, but has universal elements. If ballroom dancing seems anachronistic, it is also nostalgic, as the eighty-six countries that have joined the film's distribution list would seem to testify. Other Australian films have had dramatic success, but like theatre, timing is crucial, and *Strictly Ballroom* seems to have achieved that. It vindicates the Australian film-makers and restores confidence to an important part of our cultural development. With the film as image-maker, *Strictly Ballroom* has shown we can both entertain and perhaps even send a message of Australian spirit and independence.

Australian, Editorial, 11 September, 1992

Strictly Ballroom was developed by M&A Film Corporation Pty Ltd with the assistance of the NSW Film and Television Office and was produced with the participation of the Australian Film Finance Corporation Pty Ltd. *Strictly Ballroom* was first screened nationally in Australia in August 1992 with the following actors playing the principal roles:

SCOTT HASTINGS	Paul Mercurio
FRAN	Tara Morice
BARRY FIFE	Bill Hunter
SHIRLEY HASTINGS	Pat Thomson
LIZ HOLT	Gia Carides
LES KENDALL	Peter Whitford
DOUG HASTINGS	Barry Otto
KEN RAILINGS	John Hannan
TINA SPARKLE	Sonia Kruger
CHARM LEACHMAN	Kris McQuade
WAYNE BURNS	Pip Mushin
VANESSA CRONIN	Leonie Page
RICO	Antonio Vargas
YA YA	Armonia Benedito
TERRY	Jack Webster
KYLIE	Lauren Hewett
LUKE	Steve Grace
J.J. SILVERS	Wayne Bertram
WAITRESS	Di Emery
NATALIE	Lara Mulcahy
CLARRY	Brian M. Logan
MERV	Michael Burgess
NATHAN STARKEY	Todd McKenney
PAM SHORT	Kerry Shrimpton

Director, Baz Luhrmann
Producer, Tristram Miall
Executive Producer, Antoinette Albert
Line Producer, Jane Scott
Production Designer, Catherine Martin
Associate Production Designer, Bill Marron
Director of Photography, Steve Mason A.C.S.
Music Direction and Original Music by David Hirschfelder
Choreography, John O'Connell
Ballroom costumes designs by Angus Strathie
Editor, Jill Bilcock

PRINCIPAL CHARACTERS

SCOTT HASTINGS, aged twenty-one. Next Pan Pacific Grand Prix Champion – looks – charm – the boy with the world at his feet.

SHIRLEY HASTINGS, aged forty-five. Scott's mother, an iron-willed matriarch of the Kendall Dance Studio.

DOUG HASTINGS, aged fifty. Scott's father, intensely nervous, socially inept.

LES KENDALL, aged fifty-two. Proprietor of Kendall's Studio. Dignified, toes the Federation line. Scott's coach.

LIZ HOLT, aged nineteen. Scott's partner of fifteen years. An Anglo beauty with a nasal voice.

WAYNE BURNS, aged twenty-one. Scott's best mate and loyal supporter, no great dancer but tries hard.

VANESSA CRONIN, aged nineteen. Liz's best friend and Wayne's partner.

FRAN, aged nineteen. An awkward beginner, she has danced with a girl for two years.

NATALIE, aged nineteen. Fran's best friend and partner.

KYLIE HASTINGS, aged ten. Scott's sister.

LUKE, aged ten. Kylie's partner.

CLARRY WRENCH, aged thirty-two. A tall, gangly beginner dancer.

BARRY FIFE, aged fifty. A fleshy, sweaty man. President of the Dance Federation. The most powerful man in Ballroom Dancing.

CHARM LEACHMAN, aged forty-five. Tall, taut and sinewy. The Federation District Co-ordinator.

YA YA, aged seventy-one. Fran's Spanish grandmother.

RICO, aged forty-eight. Fran's father.

KEN RAILINGS, aged thirty-nine. A waning star desperate to make a comeback.

PAM SHORT, aged nineteen. Ken's partner.

TINA SPARKLE, aged twenty-eight. Current Pan Pacific champion.

NATHAN STARKEY, aged twenty-eight. Her partner.

TERRY BEST, aged forty-nine. Tina's coach.

J.J. SILVERS, aged fifty-seven. Master of ceremonies.

MERV, a middle-aged Federation official.

The tremolo strings of Strauss' Blue Danube Waltz can be heard as lights fade up on a red velvet stage curtain. The curtain parts to reveal in red cursive lettering the words

STRICTLY BALLROOM

A dark chord from the music and the words explode, filling the screen with white light. The light dissolves to reveal . . .

1. INT. TOWN HALL FESTIVAL NIGHT.

The slow motion silhouette of a young dancer leaps through the air. Silhouettes of couples move toward the dance floor.

2. INT. TOWN HALL. FESTIVAL NIGHT.

Last minute preparations. A number is pinned, a bow tie is adjusted and the dancers glide into their waltz. From the vantage of the onstage adjudicators' table the scrutineers look on impassively. A judge marks his card. SHIRLEY HASTINGS *cups her hands to her mouth.*

SHIRLEY: Come on a hundred!
> *Suddenly the cheers of the crowd invade the soundtrack, the music booms and the dancers accelerate into real time. Number 100* SCOTT HASTINGS *and* LIZ HOLT *are the local favourites. Valiantly they do battle with a dozen tail-suited ostrich feathered opponents. The frame freezes. Over their image the following words appear:*

SCOTT HASTINGS BALLROOM CHAMPION.

3. INT. HASTING'S HOUSE. LOUNGE ROOM. DOCO STYLE. DAY

SHIRLEY *and* DOUG *sit in front of a wall of trophies, pennants and ballroom memorabilia.* SHIRLEY *holds a framed photograph of* SCOTT.

DOUG AND SHIRLEY HASTINGS, SCOTT'S PARENTS.

SHIRLEY: [*to camera*] Scott won most of the trophies in this room – you see that's the tragedy – my son was a champion.
DOUG squirts his mouth with Cedel breath freshener.

4. INT. TOWN HALL FESTIVAL. NIGHT.

With a final flourish SCOTT *and* LIZ *finish their routine. The crowd cheers as couples leave the floor. The Master of Ceremonies,* J.J. SILVERS, *prepares to speak:*

J.J. SILVERS: Welcome to the Southern Districts . . . Waratah Championships! You're going to see some of the top dancers in the Southern Districts here today.
The crowd applaud as SCOTT *and* LIZ, *resplendent in gold sequined costumes, spin onto the floor.*

5. INT. HASTING'S HOUSE. LOUNGE ROOM. DOCO STYLE. DAY.

SHIRLEY *now sits alone.*

SHIRLEY HASTINGS, COSMETIC CONSULTANT.

SHIRLEY: [*to camera*] Well, there had been some silliness in the past – but we thought he was over it. I mean . . . we never imagined he'd do such a thing in front of . . .

6. INT. TOWN HALL. FESTIVAL. NIGHT.

J.J. SILVERS *is at the microphone.*

J.J. SILVERS: . . . Federation President, Barry Fife . . .
BARRY FIFE gives a condescending wave to the crowd.
. . . and don't forget the official Federation video, yes, the only way to dance.
BARRY, accompanied by District Co-ordinator CHARM LEACHMAN, *makes his way to the adjudicating table. He grips* LES *by the hand.*

LES: Wonderful to see you Barry.
> *J.J. SILVERS is on stage with the microphone, holding 'Barry Fife's – Dance to Win' video.*

J.J. SILVERS: Barry Fife's 'Dance to Win' is on sale here tonight . . . yeah.

7. INT. HASTING'S HOUSE. LOUNGE ROOM. DOCO STYLE. DAY.

SHIRLEY: [*to camera*] Well there was no doubt in anyone's mind that Scott and Liz would be the next Pan Pacific Grand Prix Amateur Five Dance Latin American champions. I mean they'd worked towards it all their lives. And then came that . . .

8. INT. TOWN HALL. FESTIVAL. NIGHT.

J.J. SILVERS: . . . Samba!
> *The thunder of orchestral brass, a driving Brazilian rhythm. The floor explodes into a frenzy of competing dance couples. Sequined limbs lacerate the air; burnt orange lurex, screaming red organza – the shooting star blur of diamantes in motion. Synchronised couples whip, split and crack across the floor. Amidst the cacophony of distractions, LIZ and SCOTT shine. The camera cuts to KEN RAILINGS and PAM SHORT – a couple of indeterminate age.*

9. INT. HASTING'S HOUSE. LOUNGE ROOM. DOCO STYLE. DAY.

SHIRLEY: [*to camera*] Ken Railings and Pam Short were dancing there that night..

10. INT. TOWN HALL. FESTIVAL. NIGHT.

Desperately PAM and KEN launch into a whirlwind of

evergreen variations – The El Alamein, The Peacock Shower *and* The Rio Shuffle.

11. INT. HASTING'S HOUSE. LOUNGE ROOM. DOCO STYLE. DAY.

SHIRLEY: [*to camera*] Ken's always been a wonderful ambassador for ballroom dancing – but I know everyone there that day really thought it was Scott's turn.

12. INT. TOWN HALL. FESTIVAL. NIGHT.

SCOTT and LIZ dance another spectacular variation. DOUG, FRAN, SHIRLEY, KYLIE, LUKE and others cheer excitedly.

LUKE: C'mon number 100!
> *DOUG peers through his clackety Super 8 movie camera as KYLIE cheers on her big brother.*
KYLIE: Come on number 100!
> *Suddenly KEN RAILINGS spins his partner PAM into open position, trapping SCOTT and LIZ in the corner and usurping the judges' focus.*

13. INT. KENDALL'S STUDIO. MAIN SALON. DOCO STYLE. DAY.

Coach LES KENDALL is in the studio.

LES KENDALL, SCOTT's COACH.

LES: [*to camera*] It is true, Scott and Liz became what we term 'boxed in' or 'blocked'.

14. INT. TOWN HALL. FESTIVAL. NIGHT.

SCOTT and LIZ are still trapped. KEN and PAM release their grandest variations. The judges look on approvingly.

LIZ: [*hissing through dance smile*] Piss off!

15. INT. KENDALL'S STUDIO. MAIN SALON. DOCO STYLE. DAY.

LES is in the studio.

LES: [*to camera*] . . . it was no excuse for what Scott did.

16. INT. TOWN HALL. FESTIVAL. NIGHT.

Like a warrior into battle, SCOTT *throws himself into a knee-slide between* PAM's *legs. The crowd gasp.* BARRY *hisses in* LES's *ear.*

BARRY: What the bloody hell's going on Kendall?

17. INT. KENDALL'S STUDIO. MAIN SALON. DOCO STYLE. DAY.

LES is in the studio.

LES: [*to camera*] He resorted to his own flashy crowd-pleasing steps.

18. INT. TOWN HALL. FESTIVAL. NIGHT.

SCOTT *leaps into a quick-silver spin. The crowd react.* SCOTT *extends his arm to* LIZ, *beckoning her to follow.*

SCOTT: Come on, come on!

19. INT. LIZ'S HOUSE. BEDROOM. DOCO STYLE. DAY.

LIZ sits on her bed.

LIZ HOLT, SCOTT'S PARTNER

LIZ: [*to camera*] He forced me into it – where the man goes the lady must follow – I had no choice.

8

20. INT. TOWN HALL. FESTIVAL. NIGHT.

SCOTT propels LIZ into a death-defying aerial spin. SHIRLEY's mouth is agape in horror. BARRY FIFE is purple with rage. KYLIE turns to her diminutive partner LUKE.

KYLIE: I bet you never saw that before.

21. INT. HASTING'S HOUSE. LOUNGE ROOM. DOCO STYLE DAY.

SHIRLEY: [*to camera*] I keep asking myself why? Did I do something wrong? Did I fail him as a mother? . . . in front of Barry Fife!

22. INT. TOWN HALL. FESTIVAL. NIGHT.

SCOTT and LIZ perform another startling sequence of steps. The crowd clamours for more. DOUG intently films.

23. INT. TOWN HALL FESTIVAL. NIGHT.

The crowd goes berserk as SCOTT and LIZ continue to dance their scintillating steps. BARRY is a Vesuvius about to erupt.

CHARM: [*into BARRY's ear*] I'll cut the music.
 CHARM rises. BARRY yanks her back into her seat.
BARRY: [*under his breath*] Don't be bloody stupid, woman.
 BARRY smiles as he waves to the crowd.

24. INT. KENDALL'S STUDIO. DOCO STYLE. DAY.

LES is in the studio.

LES: [*to camera*] To pick what was actually wrong with the steps, you'd have to be an experienced professional, like myself, or Federation President, Barry Fife . . .

25. INT. HASTING'S HOUSE. LOUNGE ROOM. DOCO STYLE. DAY.

SHIRLEY is distraught.

SHIRLEY: Barry Fife . . .

26. INT. BARRY FIFE'S OFFICE. DOCO.DAY.

BARRY FIFE, in his best nylon suit, is seated at a long laminex table in front of the feature wall at Federation chambers.

BARRY FIFE PRESIDENT, AUSTRALIAN DANCE FEDERATION.

BARRY: [*to camera*] Well of course, you can dance any steps you like, but that doesn't mean you'll . . .
   Slam into a close-up of BARRY's mouth.
   . . . win.

27. INT. TOWN HALL FESTIVAL. NIGHT.

J.J. SILVERS: The winners, couple No. 69, Ken Railings and Pam Short. Ken and Pam are 'Southern Star Inter-regional, New Vogue title holders', 'Putting On The Ritz, City and Country, inaugural three dance, round robin champions', 'Tulip Time Central Districts and Outlying Regions, Winter five dance two times champions' and three times 'Pan Pacific Grand Prix Amateur Five Dance Latin American champions'. Yes!
   A triumphant fanfare plays as KEN and PAM launch into their lavish sequence of bows. SCOTT defiantly holds BARRY FIFE's gaze. LIZ rushes from the floor, breaking into a run, face flushed, eyes filled with tears. SCOTT follows.

28. INT. KENDALL'S STUDIO. DOCO STYLE. DAY.

FRAN, BEGINNER DANCER.

10

FRAN: [*to camera*] I've only been dancing for two years so I haven't got a partner yet, but I thought that what they danced was wonderful. I thought they should have won.

29. INT. TOWN HALL. FESTIVAL. DAY.

As LIZ *reaches the side of the floor she is met by the well-intentioned* FRAN.

FRAN: Hi Liz! I thought you should have . . .
  LIZ's face explodes into tears as she slams past FRAN *whose glasses are knocked flying.* FRAN *bends to pick them up and rises just in time to collect* SCOTT *as he crashes through.*
SCOTT: Liz!
LIZ: [*turning on* SCOTT] Piss off!
SCOTT: Liz . . .
LIZ: Get away from me. I'm not dancing with you alright? I'm not dancing with you till you dance like you're supposed to!

30. INT. KENDALL'S STUDIO. MAIN SALON. LATE AFTERNOON.

Kendall's studio; a large slightly decrepit hall with worn but beautiful wooden floorboards. The walls are adorned with photographs and trophies from the studio's long past. DOUG *sits collecting money from arriving students.* FRAN *spreads wax flakes on the floor. A happy thirties quickstep plays.* LES *and* SHIRLEY *instruct a class of beginners.*

SHIRLEY: Keep the weight up in the chest girls . . . one, two, three.
LES: One, two, three, four . . . partner-up.
  LES *moves to partner* SHIRLEY.
SHIRLEY: [*to* LES *as they dance*] Happy as Larry they were last night . . . They were on the phone for hours.

31. INT. KENDALL'S STUDIO. KITCHEN. LATE AFTERNOON.

SCOTT and LIZ stand in the shabby Kendall's Studio kitchen.

SCOTT: I'm just asking you what you think of the steps.
LIZ: I don't think. I don't give a shit about them, we lost.

32. INT. KENDALL'S STUDIO. MAIN SALON. LATE AFTERNOON.

LES and SHIRLEY are dancing.

LES: Don't you worry about Barry . . . [*to the class*] Spinning the girl out! . . .
 LES spins SHIRLEY away from him, she comes face to face with FRAN who is still spreading wax on the floor.
SHIRLEY: [*peering at FRAN's skin*] Oh dear Fran, are you out of that apricot scrub?
FRAN: Nearly Mrs Hastings.
SHIRLEY: I'll bring some in with the toner, it's a dollar dazzler special this week
FRAN: Thanks Mrs Hastings.
LES: [*to the class*] Grand Roulette in.

33. INT. KENDALL'S STUDIO. KITCHEN. LATE AFTERNOON.

SCOTT and LIZ are arguing.

SCOTT: I don't want to end up like that drunk, Ken Railings.
LIZ: Ken Railings is a ballroom king!

34. INT. KENDALL'S STUDIO. MAIN SALON. LATE AFTERNOON.

LES spins SHIRLEY in.

LES: [*to Shirley*] I've smoothed it over. When Les Kendall

14

talks Barry Fife listens.

SHIRLEY: I've got my happy face on today, Les, everything's going to be al –

SHIRLEY is halted mid-sentence. There is a hideous cry. All heads snap towards the doorway where LIZ stands wailing like a banshee. SHIRLEY and LES, faces aghast, are frozen in dance position.

SHIRLEY/LES: Oh my God!

LIZ: [*sobbing as she stumbles towards them*] I am sorry, Mrs Hastings – I'm sorry, I've tried, God knows I've tried, but as far as I can see your son's not even interested in winning the Pan Pacifics. As of this moment, he and I are no longer partners.

SHIRLEY and LES are too shocked to react. A stunned FRAN continues to dispense an ever-increasing pile of wax.

FRAN: Hi Liz!

LIZ brushes FRAN aside, but slips on the wax and comes crashing to the floor. FRAN, in panic, bends to help LIZ but spills the box of wax on her. FRAN, desperate to make amends, hauls the struggling LIZ upright. There is a moment of equilibrium between the two girls, but suddenly FRAN's legs slip from under her and in a desperate effort to save herself, she grabs hold of LIZ's dress – ripping it and bringing LIZ crashing back to the floor.

LIZ: Vanessa!

VANESSA rushes to console the infuriated LIZ.

This stupid studio's a nightmare.

VANESSA and LIZ disappear into the change room. LES and SHIRLEY are still frozen in horror

LES: Tango please!

He and SHIRLEY launch into a tango.

Oh my God, Shirley.

SHIRLEY: Stay calm Les, stay calm. [*Catching sight of SCOTT, she motions towards DOUG*] Here he comes. Doug! Doug!

DOUG moves towards SCOTT.

DOUG: Son, can I bend your ear for a tick . . .?

15

SCOTT: Not now Dad.

> SHIRLEY *de-partners* LES *and attempts to block* SCOTT's *path.*

SHIRLEY: Don't you speak to your father like that, he's trying to talk to you – talk to him Doug!

> *But* SCOTT *has slammed into the changing-room.*

35. INT. KENDALL'S STUDIO. CHANGE ROOM. LATE AFTERNOON.

SCOTT bursts into the changing-room. WAYNE *is changing for practice.*

WAYNE: Scotty, are we going to do that Bogo Pogo?

SCOTT: Did you like the way I danced on the weekend?

WAYNE: What?

SCOTT: Did you like the way I danced on the weekend?

WAYNE: I don't know. You didn't win did you?

SCOTT: Yeah, but did you like it?

WAYNE: I don't know. Are you ready?

SCOTT: What?

WAYNE: You were going to help me and Vanessa with the Bogo Pogo.

SCOTT: I'm asking you what you thought about what I danced on the weekend.

WAYNE: I told you, I don't know.

SCOTT: Jesus, Wayne!

> SCOTT *storms out of the dressing room.* WAYNE *looks bewildered.*

36. INT. KENDALL'S STUDIO. MAIN SALON. DAY.

As SCOTT *enters the studio* LES *arrests him mid-stride and pulls him savagely into dance position. They dance through the rest of the class.*

LES: We had an agreement – Arms Clarry!

SCOTT: Maybe I changed my mind. Maybe I'm just sick of

16

dancing somebody else's steps all the time.

LES: Don't you get above yourself lad. The people who passed on those steps know a lot more about dancing than you do.

LES and SCOTT dance a silly patta-cake, patta-cake routine.

SCOTT: The audience didn't think so.

LES: [*a dismissive laugh*] Oh, the audience, the audience! – Forward on the heel Fran! – What would they know? Flashy, unusual choreography. Crowd-pleasing sure; but where was your floorcraft? – Arms Clarry! – No energy directed into the floor. Untidy feet and hands and you could have driven a truck between your left elbow – arms Clarry! – and your right hand. Do you think that's going to win you the Pan Pacific Grand Prix?

WAYNE and VANESSA tango.

WAYNE: . . . does he think that's going to win him the Pan Pacific Grand Prix?

VANESSA: He also said that what we dance is crap.

WAYNE: What?

VANESSA: Yeah, and then he ripped her dress!

LES: . . . and what's more you won't win if you don't have a partner.

SHIRLEY and the beginner CLARRY tango past.

CLARRY: Looks like Scott and Liz are still fighting Mrs H.

SHIRLEY: I'm not going to let that worry me, Clarry. I've got my happy face on today.

FRAN and NATALIE dance past. SHIRLEY squeezes FRAN's face with forced affection.

SHIRLEY: [*under her breath*] Well Fran, you managed to upset Lizzy.

FRAN: [*to NATALIE*] I'd better go and apologise.

LES is intense and sweating.

LES: Go to that little girl and beg forgiveness. You're nothing without her Scott. Remember, it takes two to tango. You've got a light in you boy – let it shine.

LIZ bursts from the changing room at precisely the moment FRAN goes to enter.

FRAN: Hi Liz!

> *FRAN is pinned between the swing door and the wall, her face pressed against the small glass window at the top of the door. LIZ stands in the doorway oblivious; red-eyed and tearful. The message is clear. To a powerful orchestral flourish from Stanley Black, SCOTT spins away from LES and snaps both arms into El Guapo position. His eyes scan the room in a slow arc, settling on LIZ. She weeping, rebuffing, refusing. He weaving, piercing, gliding. His movements are hypnotic in their intensity as he closes on the yellow canary. In range now and with the confidence a controlled body gives, he locks into a reverse spin around her. LIZ denies him. He passes again. She denies, he passes once more. Her resistance softens, her fingers reach for SCOTT. A lock; a whisk; they sweep onto the floor. The studio breathes a sigh of relief, the balance has been redressed but LIZ cannot resist a gloating giggle.*

LIZ: I knew you'd come to your senses.

> *Suddenly SCOTT, in retaliation, arrogantly throws in a combination of his own steps. The studio gasps, LIZ incensed, cannot believe her eyes. She tears herself from SCOTT. The music is silenced.*

No! I don't want this, I don't want this!

SCOTT: What do you want?

LIZ: What do I want? I'll tell you what I want. I want Ken Railings to walk in here right now and say 'Pam Short's broken both her legs and I want to dance with you'.

37. EXT. CAR INT. HIGHWAY. NIGHT.

Sound of horrifying crashing noises. Interior of a car rolling. It is as if we are peering into a tumble-drier of colourful tutus, ostrich feathers and PAM SHORT screaming.

38. INT. KENDALL'S STUDIO. MAIN SALON. NIGHT.

Fanfare as KEN RAILINGS bursts through the studio doors and strides towards LIZ.

KEN: Pam Short's broken both her legs and I want to dance with you.

Focus on LIZ's *elated face.*

KYLIE: That was unexpected.

LIZ, KEN *and the rest of the studio sweep into a Blue Danube waltz.*

LES: Thank you very much class, that's it, time to go.

SHIRLEY *bustles around packing up, trying to affect an air of normality.*

SHIRLEY: Chairs please Clarry! – Broom Natalie!

A group of dancers gather around LIZ, *as she proudly displays her new partner.*

LIZ: Ken's got his own spa bath, haven't you Ken?

KEN: Yeah, great for the aching muscles. I can get you a fantastic deal on one if you're interested.

CLARRY: Oh maybe. That'd be great Mr Railings.

SHIRLEY: Clarry – chairs.

LIZ: Ken owns Spa-orama.

SHIRLEY *storms past in the background.*

VANESSA: Wayne and I are hoping to do really well this year.

KEN: [*uninterested*] Oh yeah, great.

SHIRLEY: Fran, cups love.

WAYNE *enters.*

LIZ: Hey Wayne, come over here and meet Ken.

SHIRLEY: Kylie, feed the fish. [*Calling down the stairwell*] Doug, are you coming?

VANESSA *introduces* WAYNE.

VANESSA: He's my partner.

LIZ: [*giggles*] Fiancée.

WAYNE: G'day.

39. INT. KENDALL'S STUDIO. DOUG'S ROOM. NIGHT.

The camera tracks down the stairwell. We see a door slightly ajar. Through the door we see the 8mm projected image of SCOTT *and* LIZ *dancing their forbidden steps at the Festival.*

DOUG sits watching. The camera tracks in on DOUG's face lit by the flickering light of the projector. SHIRLEY calls again. DOUG violently snaps the projector off. DOUG's face is quivering with emotion.

SHIRLEY: Doug . . . Doug . . . Doug . . . Doug . . .

40. INT. KENDALL'S STUDIO. MAIN SALON. NIGHT.

SHIRLEY struggles to contain her emotion as she calls DOUG.

SHIRLEY: Doug! Will you hurry up please!
> *Her voice cracks, the facade crumbles and SHIRLEY stands sobbing at the top of the stairs. Suddenly the studio is quiet. All eyes turn towards the extraordinary sight of SHIRLEY HASTINGS crying. LES takes her gently by the shoulders.*
Doug?
LES: There, there, there there, where's that happy face? There, there.

41. INT. KENDALL'S STUDIO. DOUG'S ROOM. NIGHT.

We see an old black and white photograph of a young SHIRLEY striking a stylish ballroom pose. Her tail-suited partner wears the number 100. We cannot see his face. The photograph is attached to the page of a battered album. DOUG slams the album shut and places it in a corner cupboard whose neatly catalogued shelves are jammed full of photographs, film tins and ballroom memorabilia. He locks the cupboard violently with a large padlock.

42. INT. KENDALL'S STUDIO. MAIN SALON. NIGHT.

SHIRLEY sobs into LES's chest, VANESSA, KEN, LIZ and WAYNE slip quietly from the studio.

VANESSA: Come on Wayne.
LES: [*comforting SHIRLEY*] Don't worry, we're not going to give

up yet, we'll find Scott a new partner.

SHIRLEY: [*through tears*] Oh Lessie, he's my only son.

LES: I know, I know, I know. Don't worry luv, don't worry, we'll start tryouts tomorrow. Now here's Doug, he'll take you home.

> *DOUG appears from the stairwell. For a moment he watches from the shadows.*

DOUG: Come on Shirley.

LUKE: [*making for the door*] Goodnight fishes. Goodnight Uncle Les.

LES: Night, night. Sleep tight, of we go, off we go. Goodnight.

> *LES leads them to the door. He stops and leans close to SHIRLEY.*

Happy face!

> *For a moment a determined smile breaks through SHIRLEY's tears and she is gone. SCOTT enters down the backstairs. The door closes, the studio is empty. LES turns to meet SCOTT's gaze. Pause.*

LES: Scotty . . . I . . .

> *LES falters. An embarrassed silence.*

You're still our No. 1. Scott, we've got three weeks. We'll start try-outs tomorrow. We'll find you a new partner.

SCOTT: Yeah . . .

> *The camera holds on SCOTT's face. There is an echoing stamp as his shoe hits the floor.*

43. INT. KENDALL'S STUDIO. MAIN SALON. NIGHT.

It is later that night and the studio is empty. Only the light from the record player illuminates SCOTT's face. He stares through himself into the mirror and strikes a ballroom pose.

SCOTT: [*softly*] Bullshit. Bullshit!

> *SCOTT's eyes snap shut in disgust. His body sways to the driving, insistent rhythm that beats in his brain. For a moment LES's words intrude. . .*

LES: Well, to pick what was actually wrong, with the steps, you'd have to be an experienced professional, like myself.

21

. . . but they are banished by a primeval explosion of music and energy as SCOTT leaps into an inspired and savage solo. SCOTT is unaware that FRAN, concealed behind the change room door, is secret witness to this dance of dark and passionate beauty. The rhythm drives him on and on, spinning, spinning, spinning – suddenly in the mirror a face, it is FRAN. SCOTT stops, startled.

FRAN: That's looking good.

SCOTT: Uh. What are you doing here?

FRAN: I uh, I, I, I just . . .

SCOTT: How long have you been here?

FRAN: Two years – I'm just looking for someone.

SCOTT: Everyone's gone home.

FRAN: Yeah I know, It's just that I've got this idea. Like, like, I mean, it's, it's um, it's um, I wanna try to . . . I want to dance with you. I want to dance with you. I want to dance with you your way at the Pan Pacifics.

SCOTT: The Pan Pacifics? You want to dance my way at the Pan Pacifics?

FRAN: Yeah.

SCOTT: You can't dance my way. You don't win.

FRAN: It's just because you've been overdoing it. If you, if you kept it simpler, and danced from the heart.

SCOTT: What?

FRAN: And had the right partner.

SCOTT: Oh, I see, that's you, is it?

FRAN: When you dance your steps, I understand how you feel, 'cause I make up my own steps too.

SCOTT: You make up your own steps?

FRAN: Yeah – and now we both haven't got partners.

SCOTT: Look, what are you carrying on about? You've never had a partner. You've been dancing with a girl for two years, haven't you?

FRAN: Yeah . . .

SCOTT: Yeah . . .

FRAN: . . . but –

SCOTT: . . . and now you've come up to me who's been

22

dancing since I was six years old . . . and you want to dance non-Federation, and convince the judges at the Pan Pacific Grand Prix with 3 weeks to train?

FRAN: Yeah.

SCOTT: I don't think so.

FRAN: Just give me a try-out.

SCOTT: Look. Go home.

FRAN: Just one hour.

SCOTT: This is very embarrassing.

FRAN: I, I just need a chance.

SCOTT: You're going to wake up tomorrow and feel like a real idiot about this.

FRAN: Do you want to dance your own steps or not?

SCOTT: It's none of your business

FRAN: Well, do you?

SCOTT: Look. A beginner has no right to approach an Open Amateur.

FRAN: Yeah. Well an Open Amateur has no right to dance non-Federation steps . . . but you did, didn't you?

SCOTT: But that's different.

FRAN: How is it different? You're just like the rest of them. You think you're different, but you're not because you're just, you're just really scared, you're really scared to give someone new a go because you think, you know, they might just be better than you are. Well, you're just pathetic and you're gutless. You're a gutless wonder. Vivir con miedo, es como vivir a medias.

SCOTT stops, startled.

SCOTT: What's your name again?

FRAN: Fran.

SCOTT: Yeah. Fran what?

FRAN: Just Fran.

SCOTT: All right then, just Fran. Don't push me. Rumba.

SCOTT spins FRAN into dance position. She stumbles.

Great you can't even do a basic.

FRAN: You said one hour.

He takes her up again.

44. INT. KENDALL'S STUDIO MAIN SALON. NIGHT.

It is later that night. SCOTT and FRAN continue to practice.

SCOTT: One, two, three, four – one, two, three, four, one hold two, one hold two, three four, one two three four, one two three four, one two three. We're telling a story. The rumba is the dance of love. Look at me like you're in love.
    FRAN follows this instruction perhaps a little too enthusiastically.
[*taken aback*] That's it. Good.

45. INT. KENDALL'S SALON MAIN SALON. NIGHT.

Still later SCOTT works on a sequence of steps.

Turn, turn, two three four and one two three four. Good – that's it. We're going to do one basic, do a spin and then a lunge. Okay? – and – one, two and one and turn and over, one turn and lunge, one, turn and lunge. Okay. Lunge, drag pull, drag, one turn, there.
    FRAN proffers a suggestion.
FRAN: I know
SCOTT: [*ignoring her*] Wait, wait, I know, I know, we'll go – one and two.
    Again she interjects.
FRAN: Hey, we could, we –
    Again SCOTT ignores her. FRAN explodes into a flurry of flamenco steps. Silence. Close-up of an astonshed SCOTT.
SCOTT: Where did that come from?
FRAN: [*suddenly tentative*] It's a step I've been working on at home.
SCOTT: Show me?
FRAN: [*smiles*] Well. [*She begins to demonstrate.*]

46. MONTAGE. INT. KENDALL'S STUDIO. MAIN SALON DAY.

Music montage sequence. Title: The Tryouts.
LES, SHIRLEY, FRAN and the rest of the studio huddle in the kitchen looking on as SCOTT tries out with a Federation dancer.

KYLIE: She's got no body flight.

47. SHIRLEY STRIKING CALENDAR.

Close-up of a hand striking days off a calendar.

48. MONTAGE. INT. KENDALL'S STUDIO. MAIN SALON. NIGHT.

SCOTT and FRAN continue to improve.

SCOTT: Good. Stronger.

49. INT. KENDALL'S STUDIO. MAIN SALON. DAY.

SCOTT dances with TRYOUT GIRL 2. A bland Federation candidate barely distinguishable from the first. The studio members look on from the kitchen.

KYLIE: A bit of musicality please!

50. SHIRLEY STRIKING CALENDAR.

SHIRLEY is striking days off a calendar.

51. MONTAGE INT. KENDALL'S STUDIO. MAIN SALON. EARLY A.M.

SCOTT and FRAN practice before work.

SCOTT: Good. Good. Yeah, that's it, come back in, not too far.

52. INT. KENDALL'S STUDIO. MAIN SALON. DAY.

SCOTT dances with TRYOUT GIRL 3. *Another bland candidate, indistinguishable from the rest. She attempts to follow the simple routine* SCOTT *has set. The candidate looks on unconvinced. The studio looks on from the kitchen.*

FRAN: She's terrible.
They all look incredulously at FRAN.

53. SHIRLEY STRIKING CALENDAR.

SHIRLEY is striking further days off a calendar.

SHIRLEY: Either they're too tall, they're too short, they're too tubby, well you know . . .

54. INT. DOUG'S ROOM. DAY.

SHIRLEY in full Herbal Way uniform is demonstrating the 'new range' of cosmetics to FRAN *who is positioned in front of* SHIRLEY's *portable make-up mirror.*

SHIRLEY: . . . fat. It's as if he doesn't want to find anyone who's compatible.
SHIRLEY applies make-up to FRAN.
Now this one's 'Island Fantasy' . . . and that's eleven-ninety-five . . . Ah! See, that's you.
FRAN beams.

55. INT. WAYNE'S WORKPLACE. DAY.

Garage. WAYNE *degreases an engine while* CLARRY *practices the Canadian three step.*

WAYNE: He was supposed to help Vanessa and me with

that Bogo Pogo step – never even showed up.

56. INT. HAIRDRESSING SALON. DAY.

Hairdressing salon. LIZ and VANESSA apply bleaching solution to clients' hair.

VANESSA: With a guy like Scott, it could be anything. Sexuality – drugs, y'know.

57. EXT. SPA-ORAMA. DAY.

KEN and LIZ are in a portable outdoor spa bath. KEN's torso is naked, but for a fetching star-sign necklace.

KEN: He's obviously lost it sweetie. He's all washed up.
LIZ giggles.

58. INT. KENDALL'S STUDIO. MAIN SALON. NIGHT.

SCOTT and FRAN continue to practice. The fine perspiration they are covered in tells us they are hot. Things are not going well.

SCOTT: No!
They are both panting. FRAN fiddles with her glasses pushing them back into place.
FRAN: Sorry . . .
SCOTT: [cutting her off] Take a break.
SCOTT exits to the kitchen.
FRAN: How are the try-outs going?
SCOTT takes a drink from the fridge.
SCOTT: [lying] Good. Really good.
FRAN: Oh.
SCOTT returns with the drinks. Pause. An uncomfortable silence. FRAN glances at one of the old photographs which adorn the studio. It is the same as the one from DOUG's album. It shows a young SHIRLEY striking a

27

stylish ballroom pose. Her tail-suited partner has his back to us.

Your Mum and Les were really great dancers weren't they?

SCOTT: Yeah, they were.

FRAN: They don't talk about it very much.

SCOTT: No. 'cause of Dad . . . Look Fran . . .

Suddenly a loud noise from the downstairs room startles them. SCOTT switches off the light and sneaks over to the stairwell. DOUG can be seen as he carefully takes an old 78 record from his special cupboard in the downstairs room. SCOTT turns to FRAN and whispers.

The roof . . .

SCOTT and FRAN disappear into the stairwell that leads to the roof.

59. EXT. KENDALL'S STUDIO. ROOFTOP. NIGHT.

SCOTT and FRAN stand on the rooftop. The music swells up from the studio below.

FRAN: [*whispering*] What's he doing?

SCOTT: Ah, he's always hiding away doing something.

FRAN nods, and absent-mindedly removing her glasses, wipes her eye. SCOTT and FRAN's eyes connect, they hold each other's gaze.

Can you dance without those?

FRAN nods. SCOTT gently takes the glasses and puts them in his pocket.

Might help. C'mon, we've got work to do.

SCOTT and FRAN practice under a starlit night. The camera pulls out and travels down the side of the building and in through the studio window where we discover the bewildering sight of DOUG, arms in dance position, intently quick-stepping like a man possessed. We hear his faint voice counting the beat, amidst gasps for air.

28

60. EXT. KENDALL'S STUDIO ROOFTOP SUNSET MONTAGE.

Rooftop montage SCOTT and FRAN are practising against the city sunset.

61. SHIRLEY STRIKING CALENDAR.

SHIRLEY is maniacly striking more days off a calendar.

SHIRLEY: It was his year! It was his year! It was his year! It was his – year!! It was his year . . .

62. INT. HASTINGS' LOUNGE ROOM. NIGHT.

KYLIE and LUKE stand on the coffee table dressed in full Latin costume. SHIRLEY is pinning the hem of LUKE's green cat-suit pants while drinking sherry. DOUG, oblivious of physical reality, sashays and pony-hops around the room, mumbling a half-forgotten dance tune to himself.

SHIRLEY: . . . it was Scott's year, Luke. And now he's gone and thrown it all away. You wouldn't do that would you Luke?
> *LUKE shakes his head.*
LUKE: No.
DOUG: Les'll find him a partner.
SHIRLEY: There's no time, Doug. She'd have to be a champion. You think someone like Tina Sparkle's wandering around saying 'I wonder who I'll dance with?'
LUKE: Why don't you and Mrs Hastings go in the over 35's, Mr Hastings?
DOUG: [*mumbles*] I don't like the competitions.
KYLIE: Dad doesn't go in the competitions.
LUKE: But you should have a go Mr Hastings.
SHIRLEY: [*exploding*] Doug will you stop that! Stop that shuffling you stupid man.
> *SHIRLEY sinks to her haunches, racked by tears.*

I can't bear it. I just can't bear it.

KYLIE: [*comforting her mother*] Don't cry Mum. Scott'll find a new partner. Don't worry, he will.

63. INT. KENDALL'S STUDIO. NIGHT.

At the closing bars of SCOTT and FRAN's theme, they complete their final sequence. There is silence. SCOTT smiles.

SCOTT: You're ready.

FRAN: What for?

SCOTT: I want you and me to tryout for Les tomorrow night.

FRAN: At the State? Really?

SCOTT: Yep.

> *FRAN yells in triumph and jumps in the air. She is barely able to contain her excitement. SCOTT laughs and playfully draws her to him.*

64. EXT. KENDALL'S STUDIO. NIGHT.

The little studio nestles under a starlit sky. The silhouette of the two dancers flickers in the lighted window. As the camera pulls out the rooftop comes into view with the solitary figure of DOUG amidst his mysterious manic shuffling.

65. EXT. TOLEDO MILK-BAR – FRAN'S HOME. NIGHT.

SCOTT and FRAN walk through the industrial area of the city. The glow of the factories illuminates the night sky.

SCOTT: [*struggling with the pronunciation*] Vivir con miedo es como vivir . . . a . . . a . . .

FRAN: [*correcting him*] Vivir a medias.

SCOTT: [*better this time*] Vivir con miedo, es como vivir a medias.

FRAN: Yeah, um . . . 'To live with fear is like to half live' – I mean – 'is a life half lived.'

32

SCOTT: [*unsure*] Oh yeah, like a proverb?

FRAN: Yeah. Sort of.

SCOTT: A life half lived, I like it.

> *SCOTT and FRAN have arrived outside the run down Toledo milk-bar. They stand in silence, unsure. The sounds of night envelope them.*

SCOTT: Well . . . I'll see you at the State tomorrow.

FRAN: Okay, do you, do you think the rumba's the right one to do?

SCOTT: Yeah, Les'll love it.

FRAN: I do too . . . the rumba I mean.

> *Pause.*

SCOTT: Fran, you know when I said about the rumba, being y'know the dance of love.

FRAN: [*expectantly*] Yeah.

SCOTT: Well . . .

FRAN: Yeah . . .

SCOTT: It's pretend. You just pretend to be in love, it's not real.

FRAN: [*covering*] Oh, no I didn't 'cause you didn't, ah . . .

> *FRAN collides with a stack of boxes filled with beer cans, they clatter noisily to the ground.*

SCOTT: Are you alright?

> *Suddenly the exterior light clicks on. FRAN looks worriedly towards the milk-bar.*

FRAN: You'd better go. I'll see you tomorrow.

SCOTT: Okay.

> *She hurries away.*

66. INT. FRAN'S HOUSE. ROOM BEHIND TOLEDO MILK-BAR. NIGHT.

FRAN's grandmother, YA YA, sews on an old treadle machine by the light of a black and white television. At the sound of the front door, she stops, listening to footsteps down the pathway. Trouble. FRAN moves furtively through the darkened living room. Suddenly FRAN stops, startled. RICO enters from the kitchen. He's short with a swarthy,

33

unshaven face. Pause. There is a moment of tension.

RICO: Francisca, ¿Cómo vienes tan tarde? [*Why are you so late?*]

FRAN: Estuve ensayando con Natalia [*I've been practising with Natalie.*]

RICO: Manana por la noche te necesito aquí para la fiesta. [*Tomorrow night I need you here for the fiesta.*]

FRAN: Tengo que ir a ensayar. [*I have to go to dancing.*]

RICO: Tú sales demasiao. Manana te quedas aquí. [*You are out too much. Tomorrow you stay here.*]

FRAN: Pero [*But*]... tomorrow we have the State Championships.

RICO: Ya está bien! Manana te quedas aquí. [*Enough! Tomorrow you stay here.*]

> *FRAN defiantly holds her father's gaze. RICO shakes his head and muttering, moves out to the verandah. FRAN goes to her bedroom. YA YA watches her with concern.*

67. INT. STATE CHAMPIONSHIPS. RSL CLUB. MAIN HALL. NIGHT.

'The Australian Federation presents: Night Of A Thousand Stars – State Championships'. A stunningly tall gazelle-like girl, is being introduced on-stage, prior to taking the floor at the State Festival. She removes her silk cape to reveal a beautiful body, near naked but for the shimmering decoration that is her costume. The music would serve as appropriate accompaniment to 'Venus rising from the waves'. The crowd applaud rapturously.

J.J. SILVERS: The State Championships, featuring the magical Mr Nathan Starkey and Miss Tina Sparkle.

68. INT. STATE CHAMPIONSHIPS. RSL CLUB. RESTAURANT. NIGHT.

A dining table around which BARRY, LES, CHARM, TERRY and

34

four other Federation heavies sit. The restaurant is on the mezzanine level of the RSL Club which hosts the State Championships. Through the glass window which backs the diners we can see the preliminary heats of the championship under way.

BARRY: I want Tina to be Scott's new partner, Les.

LES: Tina Sparkle?

BARRY: That's right Les. Bloody Nathan is going to announce his retirement tonight. Scott and Tina are both without partners and I think it would be advantageous for all concerned if they were seen together.

    MERV, a middle-aged Federation official interjects.

MERV: But Barry, Scott's shenanigans have caused a lot of distracting chat down our way.

BARRY: That's why it's important Scott's seen to be dancing the right steps with the right partner Merv.

    TERRY, TINA's winsome coach chimes in.

TERRY: Dance sport needs good young couples, Merv.

BARRY: Terry's hit the nail on the head, Merv. Let's not start chucking the babies out with the bathtub.

LES: [*struggling to contain his excitement*] I'm a hundred percent behind it Barry.

69. INT. TOLEDO MILK-BAR. NIGHT.

YA YA is cooking a hamburger on the sizzling hotplate. NATALIE and FRAN hurry past.

FRAN: Estare de vuelta en una hora. Voy a ayudar a Natalia a mudarse. [*I'll only be an hour, I'm helping Natalie move.*]

    YA YA shrugs her shoulders — it is enough for FRAN and she is off.

YA YA: Francisca.

    FRAN stops.

No vuelvas tarde. [*Don't come back late.*]

    FRAN goes. YA YA smiles to herself.

70. INT.STATE CHAMPIONSHIPS. RSL CLUB. RESTAURANT. NIGHT.

The meal is over. BARRY rises from the table, as do the rest of the gathering.

BARRY: [*with a good natured belch*] Well Gentlemen – let's make this a bloody good festival.
> *Everyone shakes hands.*
Oh Les, just a tick.
> *BARRY takes LES by the shoulder and guides him away from the group.*
LES: This is wonderful Barry, wonderful.
BARRY: He doesn't deserve her Les. I've been fielding phone calls all week about the steps Scott danced at that Festival.
LES: Scott's learnt his lesson Barry, he's changed.
BARRY: We both know exactly where that young man was heading. Don't we? Foolish boy, [*He stops and looks LES in the eye*] but Scott's got his second chance. Let's not forget, Les, that a Pan Pacific Champion becomes a hero, a guiding light to all dancers. Someone who'll set the right example.
> *Out in the auditorium amidst the ocean of coloured ostrich feathers, senior couples glissade and strut through the finals of the 'Barclay Blues.' WAYNE and VANESSA are also trying their hearts out. KEN and LIZ are not dancing well. KEN's eyes are glazed and he sweats profusely. He blows another step.*
LIZ: [*through forced smile*] You've been drinking!
KEN: [*through gritted smile*] Bullshit! Push it!
LIZ: You bloody have!
> *Back in the restaurant BARRY and LES halt at the window which overlooks the dance floor. As BARRY takes in the festival, a single tear streaks his cheek.*
BARRY: I love dancing Les, and I'm not going to let what we've fought for all these years be destroyed.
LIZ: Drunk, aren't ya.

KEN: Bullshit, Bullshit.

LIZ: You bloody are. Get your head up.

> *SHIRLEY walks through the crowd to KYLIE, LUKE and DOUG.*

SHIRLEY: Do you two know anything about this girl Scott's trying out with?

> *LUKE shakes his head.*

KYLIE: Who is it, Mum?

SHIRLEY: Oh goodness, I'd be the last one to know. Scott says we'll never guess.

> *The 'Barclay Blues' concludes, the crowd applaud. As the couples leave the floor, LES arrives looking flustered.*

71 . INT. STATE CHAMP/SHIPS. RSL CLUB. CHANGE ROOM. NIGHT.

CLARRY is adjusting his tie in the mirror. SCOTT approaches.

SCOTT: Hey, Clarry, you haven't seen Fran, have you?

CLARRY: No, maybe she got a lift with Natalie. It's our first big comp today.

72. INT. STATE CHAMPIONSHIPS. RSL CLUB. NIGHT.

LES joins SHIRLEY, WAYNE, KYLIE, LUKE, DOUG and VANESSA.

SHIRLEY: Les, do you know anything about this girl?

LES: Jesus, news travels fast around this place.

KYLIE: Who is it, Uncle Les?

LES: You silly sourpusses! Have a look at this.

> *The camera cuts to a spinning headline shot. It zooms in tight on the page. A slash of light illuminates the copy: TINA SPARKLE UP FOR GRABS – NATHAN TO RETIRE.*

> *The group excitedly crowd round SHIRLEY as she reads:*

SHIRLEY: Three times Pan Pacific Champion, Tina Sparkle, is hunting for a new partner. It was announced today, her partner of . . . ten years, Nathan Starkey, will be retiring because of commitments to his landscape gardening business. Their farewell exhibition will be at this weekend's State Finals. The question on every dance fans lips is, 'who will snaffle Tina?'.

LES: Scott Hastings, that's who.

SHIRLEY: Oh my god. Tina Sparkle.

SHIRLEY's eyes fill spontaneously with tears of joy.
Les do you think she will dance with him?

LES: Straight after her exhibition, she's hopping into the social dance with Scott.

SHIRLEY: Oh Doug, it's an answer to our prayers.

DOUG: She's a nice little chickie. She photographs well.

DOUG films FRAN who has quietly arrived.

SHIRLEY: Oh Franny, isn't it exciting?

FRAN: [*unclear*] Oh . . .

SHIRLEY: I thought he'd never find a new partner. Everything's turned out wonderfully.

FRAN: [*tentatively*] Do you think so?

SHIRLEY: Of course I do! Les and I are beside ourselves.

FRAN: Well, I'm very happy too.

SHIRLEY: 'Course you are luvvy. Gee you look nice tonight. [*Conspiratorially*] You've been using that buff puff I gave you, haven't you.

LES: [*elbowing FRAN*] If he doesn't hurry up I might just jump in there myself.

FRAN punches LES playfully on the arm.

FRAN: Oh, Mr Kendall . . .

All look at FRAN strangely. SCOTT arrives and sees FRAN smiling surrounded by the group.

SCOTT: Oh, Mum . . . I was going to tell you . . .

SHIRLEY: Oh yes, very funny, you little devil. Well, we know all about it.

WAYNE: [*slapping SCOTT on the shoulder*] Bloody fantastic, mate.

VANESSA: You should have told us, you know.

FRAN is blushing.

LES: Well, Uncle Lessy was onto it first.

SCOTT: You haven't even seen us dance yet.

LES: C'mon son. You two were made for each other.

DOUG: [*showing* FRAN *his camera*] You find it difficult to get the films now – it's all video, video, video.

SHIRLEY: For goodness sake Doug! She's not the slightest bit interested. Look at her, she's beside herself. Oh, who would have thought it eh? Our Scott dancing with someone like Tina Sparkle.

> *FRAN goes cold. She fights the tears.* J.J. SILVERS *can be heard over the microphone.*

J.J. SILVERS: Yes! The fairy princess of the dance floor . . . Miss Tina Sparkle and for the last time, current Pan Pacific Grand Prix, amateur five dance Latin American champion, Mr Nathan Starkey!

FRAN: [*weakly*] Tina Sparkle . . .

> *The crowd go wild.* NATHAN STARKEY *and* TINA SPARKLE *twirl onto the floor in a hail of applause. They are splendidly dressed in magnificent Latin costumes made entirely of tiny plastic fruit.* FRAN *is about to give way to her emotion.* SCOTT *struggles with the words.* SHIRLEY, *applauding, leers into* FRAN's *face.*

SHIRLEY: Oh, isn't Tina beautiful!

> *She forces* SCOTT's *attention back to the floor.*

J.J. SILVERS: [*through deafening applause*] Ladies and Gentlemen, this evening, dancing together for the last time, Mr Nathan Starkey and Miss Tina Sparkle. What a great partnership and what a shame, as they dance for you the Fruity Rumba.

> SCOTT *is looking back to* FRAN, *but she has gone.*

SHIRLEY: [*to* SCOTT] She's a funny girl!

> *The music blares, the Fruity Rumba begins.*

SCOTT: [*to* SHIRLEY] Be back in a minute.

J.J. SILVERS: Oh, they're beginning with a double ronde shuffle. Yes, give them a round of applause. Well deserved.

> FRAN *pushes her way through the crowd.* LIZ *and* KEN *are arguing beside the dance floor.* FRAN *collides with* LIZ, *who turns sharply and seeing the beginner exclaims.*

LIZ: Watch it Frangipani!

From FRAN's *point of view* LIZ's *sneering face looms large. As* FRAN *flees* KEN *and* LIZ *argue.* KEN *drinks from a metal thermos.*

KEN: Listen Sweetie, I'm the one driving the engine around here, alright?

LIZ: Well if you're driving the engine, what's that in the thermos?

SCOTT, in pursuit of FRAN, *now collides with* LIZ. LIZ *turns sharply but her manner changes when she sees* SCOTT.

[*smiling sweetly*] Hi Scott!

SCOTT: Have you seen Fran?

KEN: Fran, Fran. Who?

J.J. SILVERS: It's a double dip . . . ah! . . . into a quick whip split. Beaut! Oh, yes, a beautifully arched crescent moon that will go down a treat with the judges at the Pan Pacific this year.

On the main floor. NATHAN *and* TINA *are performing before a hushed audience.*

Oh, yes it's classic Fife. A twilight lift.

SHIRLEY/LES: [*to* KYLIE *and* LUKE] Do you know where Scott went?

All four push through the crowd.

SHIRLEY/LES/KYLIE/LUKE: Excuse me, excuse me, excuse me. excuse me.

73. INT. STATE CHAMPIONSHIPS. RSL CLUB. BACKSTAGE NIGHT.

SCOTT *runs backstage.* FRAN *hides in the shadows. She knows he is there. He looks to the floor and slowly speaks.*

SCOTT: Fran, I didn't know anything about that.

FRAN: Are you going to dance with Tina?

SCOTT *searches for an answer.*

SCOTT: I . . . she's a champion.

FRAN: I think you should; she's your style; you'd really suit each other.

SCOTT: I've been working towards winning the Pan Pacifics since I was six years old.

> *FRAN turns, the light catches her face. FRAN looks towards NATHAN and TINA, the Federation couple float surrealistically in a shimmering mirage of white light.*

FRAN: I'm sure you will win.

> *SCOTT follows FRAN's gaze. He can see the vision of NATHAN and TINA. Like the child seeing the emperor's new clothes, he realises there is nothing there.*

. . . I could never do that.

> *Slowly, he looks back to FRAN. Their eyes connect. There is music, and they are dancers. The distance between them disappears. They become one, dancing out the simple, profound, ancient beauty of the real Cuban rumba. Backstage, couples making their way to and from the dressing rooms stop to watch SCOTT and FRAN. They both now dance the dance of love with arresting sincerity. More and more people are seduced away from the floor-show, drawn by the physical intensity between SCOTT and FRAN. As LES, SHIRLEY, DOUG, KYLIE and LUKE move backstage they see a small crowd of people, backs turned to the main event, gathering around the shadowy figures of two lone dancers. At the onstage scrutineers table CHARM notices the disturbance. Discreetly she alerts BARRY FIFE. The shocked faces of LES, SHIRLEY and DOUG are seen as they discover the focus of the onlookers. KYLIE and LUKE weave their way through the spectators' legs to the front of the crowd.*

KYLIE: It's the inconceivable sight of Scott dancing with Fran.

> *At the scrutineers table BARRY puts his mouth to CHARM's ear.*

BARRY: Check it out.

> *CHARM leaves. LIZ is pushing her way through the crowd. On the floor the Fruity Rumba finale is taking place with TINA being held high. As SCOTT and FRAN*

come into view LIZ *makes an involuntary exclamation of disgust.*

LIZ: You're kidding!

From FRAN's *point of view* LIZ's *face is seen, contorted by outrage and disdain. Suddenly* FRAN *becomes conscious of the crowd, her confidence wanes. She is seized by fear, her old awkwardness returns and she comes crashing to the floor. A kick of shock resounds through the onlookers. There is a strange taut silence. The camera holds on* FRAN's *mortified expression, her face is flushed with shame. The distant applause for* TINA *and* NATHAN *breaks the moment.* SHIRLEY *galvanises into action as* SCOTT *bends to help* FRAN. *The pair are pulled apart by* SHIRLEY *and* LES.

LES: Quick, Tina's coming.

SHIRLEY: [*with urgency*] I'll give you a hand Fran.

SCOTT: Mum, I'm gonna take . . .

SHIRLEY: No. no – no I'm helping Fran, I don't want to hear it. Les, give me a hand.

SHIRLEY and LIZ *help* FRAN *up –* NATHAN *and* TINA *burst backstage.*

LES: [*covering*] Tina, wonderful, wonderful . . . the fruit . . . everything!

CHARM *arrives on the scene.*

CHARM: Les, President Fife would like a word with you and Scott – in the Servery, now.

She turns on her heel and is off.

TINA: [*looking at* FRAN] What's going on?

SHIRLEY: Ah, silly accident; this poor girl fell. [*SHIRLEY offers her hand*] I'm Shirley Hastings. . .

SCOTT: Mum . . .

LES: [*forcing* SCOTT's *attention back to* TINA] Scott, Tina's been dying to meet you.

SCOTT: Hello Tina – look mum.

SHIRLEY: No, no Scott, we'll look after Fran. You need to have a chat with President Fife.

LES: [*dragging him away*] Better not keep him waiting. We'll be back for the social Tina. Take your time getting changed. Scott!

KEN: [*approaching* TINA] Top routine Teens.

    TINA *looks blankly.* KYLIE *turns to* LUKE.

KYLIE: I thought that was good.

74. INT. STATE CHAMPIONSHIPS. RSL. GIRLS' CHANGE ROOM. NIGHT

FRAN *is being ushered into the changing-room by* SHIRLEY. LIZ *and* VANESSA *follow.*

SHIRLEY: Come on, come on.

FRAN: Mrs Hastings, . . .

SHIRLEY: [*cutting her off*] I don't know what you two thought you were doing. There's obviously been a whole lot of things going on – but we're going to fix that nasty bruise and then, Fran, I think it would be best for everyone if you went home.

FRAN: But, we were . . .

LIZ: You're a beginner Fran. What the hell did you think you were doing?

VANESSA: And you're really clumsy, that's why you fell over.

FRAN: Scott wanted . . .

SHIRLEY: Well of course Scott would say that, but you don't want to ruin his chances do you?

    FRAN *hesitates.*

Do you? Now you can see it'd be best for everybody concerned if you just went home and forgot all about this, can't you Franny?

    FRAN *cannot answer.*

Can't you?

FRAN: [*close to tears*] Yes, Mrs Hastings.

75. INT. STATE CHAMPIONSHIPS. RSL CLUB. KITCHEN. NIGHT.

A stark, fluorescent-lit industrial kitchen. Billows of steam emanate from the giant dish-washing machine. BARRY's face is pushed up hard against SCOTT's.

BARRY: I understand Les has lined you up with Tina Sparkle. Don't blow it son, 'cause if you don't start listening to your teachers and superiors there won't be a mark on the scorecard low enough for you at the Pan Pacifics. Comprende?

LES: [*chiming in*] Barry's only thinking of your well–being.

BARRY: Where do you think we'd be if everyone went around making up their own steps?

SCOTT: Out of a job.

    SCOTT turns on his heel and strides from the kitchen.

LES: [*horrified*] Don't listen to him Barry. He, he, he's excited because he's going to dance with Tina. He, he doesn't know what he's saying. Scott! Scott!

76. INT. STATE CHAMPIONSHIPS. RSL CLUB. GAMES ROOM. NIGHT.

SHIRLEY rushes to reassure TERRY, TINA's coach.

TERRY: Now we can't expect Tina to wait around all night Shirley.

SHIRLEY: Yes, I know Terry, I'm sorry.

TERRY: Oh, look.

    TINA enters in yet another remarkable costume.

SHIRLEY: Oh, Tina, oh my goodness, you look terrific.

    WAYNE arrives on the scene.

WAYNE: [*to SHIRLEY*] What the hell was that all about?

SHIRLEY: What?

WAYNE: You know with Fran?

SHIRLEY: [*covering with laughter*] Fran . . . Fran . . .

TINA: Fran?

SHIRLEY: Fran . . . Fran . . .

TINA: Fran, wasn't she that girl that ah . . .

SHIRLEY: [*laughing*] Well, here we all are!

    SCOTT strides towards the group.

SCOTT: Where is she?

SHIRLEY: Who?

SCOTT: Fran.

SHIRLEY: Fran, Fran, Fran who?

TINA: You know, the girl that fell.

SHIRLEY: [*laughing*] Oh, she went home, darling. Don't worry about her.

SCOTT: What?

VANESSA: She went shopping, Scott.

LIZ: [*giggling*] No. She had to make a phone call.

SCOTT: You're pathetic.

WAYNE: What's wrong with you?

SCOTT: That's what I've been trying to find out for the last three weeks. Wayne. What is wrong with me! What is so wrong with the way I dance?

SHIRLEY laughs nervously

LES: C'mon now Scott. Tina's waiting.

SCOTT: You're all so scared you wouldn't know what you thought.

TERRY: Look is he dancing with Tina or not?

SCOTT: I'm sorry Tina, I'm not available.

TERRY is flabbergasted.

TERRY: Well . . .

SCOTT turns and begins to run towards the exit.

SHIRLEY: No, Scott, wait . . . Wayne. Wayne!

WAYNE moves to block SCOTT's exit.

WAYNE: Scott . . .

WAYNE is brushed aside by a determined SCOTT. He watches SCOTT disappear through the Golden Archway of the Games Room. TINA is absolutely lost.

TINA: Look, what's going on?

KEN, not one to miss an opportunity, offers his arm with a capped tooth smile.

KEN: Care for a dance, Teens?

77. EXT. STREET. NIGHT.

SCOTT runs through the darkened streets.

45

78. INT. STATE CHAMPIONSHIPS. RSL CLUB. GAMES ROOM. NIGHT.

As WAYNE *makes his way through the corridors of the Festival,* BARRY *snaffles him with a pointed finger.*

BARRY: Jeez, you danced impressively today.

WAYNE: [*taken aback*] You think so, Mr Fife?

BARRY: Oh God yes. You should try a Bogo Pogo in your samba though. It's a terrific step, especially coming out of a Lock-Whisk.

WAYNE: Yeah. Well, actually Mr Fife . . .

BARRY: It's in me video, you got one?

WAYNE: Ah well no.

BARRY: [*producing a video from his pocket*] Here take this one.

WAYNE: Gee thanks Mr Fife.

BARRY: [*nodding sagely*] Y'know Scott's not the only one with a future to think about – it's Wayne isn't it? Yeah I've seen this bad influence before, Wayne. You know one bad egg can rot the whole barrel. Know what I mean?
    Enormous close up of BARRY's *eye as he winks at* WAYNE.

79. EXT. TOLEDO MILK-BAR. NIGHT.

Panting SCOTT *halts outside the run-down milk-bar. It is closed. He raps on the glass door. There is no response.*

80. EXT. TOLEDO MILK-BAR. SIDE ALLEY. NIGHT.

Warily SCOTT *makes his way down the side alley. Through a crack in the gate he can make out a backyard where a small party is in progress. The revellers are silhouetted against the flicker of an open fire and the sound of music and laughter drifts through the night.*

81. EXT. TOLEDO MILK-BAR. BACKYARD SIDE PASSAGE. NIGHT.

SCOTT cautiously opens the gate and makes his way down the side passage. He can see FRAN moving around the edges of the party. SCOTT creeps down beside the house to where the shadows end and the firelight begins. SCOTT grabs FRAN's arm and pulls her into the shadows.

SCOTT: Fran.

FRAN: [*startled whisper*] What are you doing here?

SCOTT: I want to dance with you.

FRAN: Go away. I'll get in trouble.

SCOTT: What happened to a life lived in fear and all that stuff?

FRAN: It's no use. You were right, I'm a beginner. I'll never be like them.

SCOTT: I don't want you to be like them – you're better than all of them.

    Pause.

Fran, I want to dance with you. At the Pan Pacifics.

FRAN: We won't win.

SCOTT: I just want to dance our steps.

    There is a moment of stillness between the pair. They are very close now, almost touching. Suddenly, RICO appears.

RICO: Francisca . . . [*he breaks off when he sees SCOTT*] quien es este? [*Who is this?*]

    FRAN looks from RICO to SCOTT and back to RICO.

FRAN: Es . . . [*This is*] . . . This is my dancing partner.

RICO: [*to SCOTT*] You go now.

SCOTT: But . . .

RICO: [*suddenly angry*] Vete! Vete! [*Go! Go!*] Go! Go!

SCOTT: We just dance together, that's all.

    There is a pause. Conversations taper off as people turn their eyes in the direction of SCOTT and RICO.

RICO: What dance do you dance so late at night?

    The party has stopped, all eyes are now upon SCOTT.

He looks to the crowd and then back to RICO. SCOTT
*looks at a faded bull-fighting poster on the verandah
wall.*

SCOTT: **Paso doble.**

Suddenly the diminutive YA YA *appears and rushes
towards* SCOTT.

YA YA: [*as she jabs at* SCOTT] **Tú? Tú bailas pasodoble? Tú
bailas pasodoble?** [*You? You dance the paso doble? You
dance the paso doble?*]

SCOTT: **What?**

YA YA: **Tú bailas,** [*You dance*] **You danca paso doble?**

SCOTT: **Yeah.**

YA YA: [*she claps her hands*] **Show! Show!**

*YA YA prods SCOTT and FRAN towards the verandah and
into the ring of spectators. She prods again.* **Show!**
*RICO looks to YA YA confused, then a smile passes his
lips.*

RICO: [*a public announcement*] **Yes, we want to see this
paso doble. Venga, a ver ese pasodoble!** [*We want to see
this paso doble!*]

*A murmur goes through the crowd; 'The paso doble, the
paso doble.'*

**Come on show us your paso doble. Show me your
pasodoble.**

From SCOTT's *point of view there is a ring of hostile
faces. Someone produces a guitar.* RICO's *challenge is
punctuated by a flourish of strings.* SCOTT *has an
inward smile of confidence as he accepts the challenge.*
FRAN *is reluctant, but* SCOTT *spins her onto the
verandah. The night is still with expectation.*

SCOTT: [*an encouraging whisper*] **It's alright, just try and
keep up.** [*To guitarist*] **Four count intro.**

*He stamps the floor, striking a dramatic pose. He winks
at FRAN and they both dash across the floor in their
paso, SCOTT clicking his fingers and stamping his feet.
There is a moment of stunned silence and then the
spectators begin to chuckle. YA YA's expression is
bewildered. SCOTT, fighting the reaction, drives the*

*dance stronger and stronger, but the laughter increases
to a raucous howling.* SCOTT *breaks off into a temper.*
What . . . what's so funny?

The laughter dies to a still tension. RICO *looks to* YA YA,
slowly rises and walks to SCOTT.

RICO: [*into* SCOTT'*s face*] Paso doble? [*He looks to* YA YA *who
joins him*] Paso doble!

*RICO's slouching body snaps into the taut frame of a
matador. His black eyes fix on the bull. To the rhythmic
clapping of the onlookers, he and* YA YA *begin to dance.
He the matador, she the cape.* YA YA'*s comic shuffle has
disappeared. They dance with dignity and strength.
The guitarist accompanies them. A final stamp to
'Olé's', everyone claps and cheers.* SCOTT *is awe-struck.*
RICO *gestures toward* SCOTT.

[*to* FRAN]: Así pierdes tú el tiempo? [*This is what you
waste your time on?*]

YA YA: [*instructing, as she moves towards the couple*] El
Cachondo podrá mover el culo, pero lo que es de ritmo,
no tiene ni puñetera idea. [*Hot stuff, might be able to
shake his tail feather, but he knows chicken shit about
rhythm.*]

FRAN: [*to* SCOTT] Grandma would like to teach us.

RICO: Falta le hace. [*He needs it.*]

SCOTT still dazed, nods. YA YA *begins to unbutton*
SCOTT'*s shirt, exposing his bare chest and stomach.*

YA YA: Bonito cuerpo. Vamos a ver, donde sientes tu el
ritmo? [*Nice body. Where do you feel the rhythm?*]

FRAN: Where do you feel the rhythm?

SCOTT stamps his feet.

YA YA: No No!

She plants her hands on SCOTT'*s stomach and heart.*

No, Aquí, aquí! [*No, here, here.*]

She nods to RICO. *He metres a beat on his guitar body.*
YA YA *begins to beat a counter rhythm on* SCOTT'*s heart
and chest. It makes a good sound.*

Listen to the rhythm, don't be scared. Acompáname.
[*Follow*]

FRAN: Follow.

> SCOTT *does so, strengthening the sound with his own hands.* RICO *moves onto the floor. The spectators join in the rhythm. It is infectious. The room is shaking with rhythm, and* SCOTT *and* RICO *are the central drum.*

82. EXT. TOLEDO MILK-BAR. REAR VERANDAH. LATER NIGHT.

The room is exploding. All involved, all singing, all dancing. It is stirring, strong and free. An irrepressible rhythm, a party, a lesson, a religious experience – the paso doble. SCOTT *and* RICO *throw their heads back with the final beat of the music. The revellers clap and cheer the united* SCOTT *and* RICO. FRAN *looks on smiling.*

83. INT. HASTINGS' HOUSE. KITCHEN/LOUNGE ROOM. NIGHT.

SHIRLEY sits at the kitchen table, sewing. SCOTT enters.

SHIRLEY: [*rising*] Have you eaten? If you haven't, there's some chops in the fridge.

SCOTT: No, I'm fine.

SHIRLEY: [*exploding*] How could you? How could you do that to Tina? She's a Pan Pacific champion.

SCOTT: Mum . . .

SHIRLEY: First thing tomorrow morning, you'll get on that telephone and apologise.

SCOTT: I won't be dancing with Tina.

SHIRLEY: What!

SCOTT: I'm dancing with Fran.

SHIRLEY: Fran!

> DOUG *appears in his pyjamas and* KYLIE *pokes her head around the corner.*

Doug, he said he won't be dancing with Tina.

DOUG: I heard.

SHIRLEY: Well do something about it, you silly man!

SCOTT: Why do you pick on dad all the time?

SHIRLEY: How dare you talk to me like that! The sacrifices we've made for you, the money, the time and effort . . .

SCOTT: Shut up!

SHIRLEY: And what about Les? He's taught you everything you know, and you're just throwing it back in his face.

SCOTT: I'm bored with it!

SHIRLEY: I don't believe I'm hearing this . . . I've been with your father for twenty-five years. Do you think I get bored? Of course I do. But you stick with your goals and eventually they bring their own rewards.

SCOTT: What rewards?

SHIRLEY: Winning the Pan Pacific!

SCOTT: I don't care about winning the Pan Pacific!

> SHIRLEY slaps SCOTT's face.

84. INT. KENDALL'S STUDIO. MAIN SALON. DAY.

LES is distraught.

LES: He doesn't care about winning the Pan Pacific Grand Prix?

SHIRLEY: That's what he said. He just wants to dance his silly steps with Fran.

WAYNE: Well that's great for the studio isn't it?

SHIRLEY: Wayne, don't let your imagination run away with itself.

WAYNE: It's true, Mrs H. It's like President Fife says – 'one bad egg can rot the whole barrel'.

> *DOUG pumps Cedel breath freshener into his mouth.*

SHIRLEY: No, you're all overreacting. Nothing bad is going to happen . . .

> *Suddenly the blood chilling howl of a wounded animal invades the sound track. All eyes snap to the doorway where LIZ stands howling like a banshee.*

What?

LIZ: [*near hysteria*] Ken dropped me!

> *SHIRLEY looks to LES. They both look to DOUG as he*

52

stands desperately pumping breath freshener into his mouth.

85. INT/EXT. TOLEDO MILK-BAR. BACK VERANDAH. DAY.

FRAN stands on the coffee table dressed in the silk underskirts of YA YA's flamenco dress. YA YA pins the hem as FRAN squirms uncomfortably. SCOTT and RICO practice the paso doble.

YA YA: Estáte quieta. Esto se arregla. [*Stand still, we'll fix it.*]

FRAN: People will laugh at me.

YA YA: Acuérdate: 'Vivir con miedo' . . . [*Remember: A life lived with fear . . .*]

FRAN: [*completing the sentence*] ' . . . es como vivir a medias'. Yo lo sé abuela [*. . . is a life half lived. I know Grandma.*]

YA YA: Cuando tu madre salía al escenario, lo llenaba aunque llevara sólo trapos. [*Your mother could wear a potato sack and still light up the stage.*]

FRAN: [*mumbling*] Claro, porque era muy guapa . . . [*She was beautiful . . .*]

YA YA: Tú puedes serlo tanto o más, créeme. [*You can be just as beautiful believe me.*]

FRAN: No . . .

YA YA: Yes – you just got to not be scared. Mira [*Look*] [*YA YA snips the hem*] El vestido seguro que va a quedar mono, pero el resto depende de ti. Vale? [*We'll make this dress nice o.k, then after that it's up to you. Alright?*] Alright?

   FRAN nods. YA YA looks into her grand-daughter's eyes.
You remind me of your mother, y'know. I'm very proud of you and if your mum was here, she would be very proud too.

RICO: [*demonstrating*] Francisca. Francisca. It's too jazzy. Don't throw away your energy.

Absent-mindedly RICO *pulls* FRAN *down from the coffee table.*

[*partnering* FRAN] See, keep the focus between you. The face, strong.

FRAN follows RICO *in a complicated piece of footwork.* RICO *looks up, surprised. A moment between father and daughter.*

Un, Dos, Tres. Muy bien. [*Good Fran, good – very good.*] *They continue to dance.*

Así, así. [*Yes, yes!*]

The rhythm builds and underscores the following section.

86. INT/EXT TOLEDO MILKBAR. BACK VERANDAH. EVENING.

SCOTT *and* FRAN *practice. The rhythm is beaten out by* YA YA *with a mop.*

Spinning headline shot: NEW STEPS RUMOURED.

87. INT. WEEKEND FESTIVAL FOYER. DAY.

Close-up of a GIRL *in ballroom costume.*

GIRL: [*to camera*] New steps . . .

Spinning headline shot: NEW STEPS RUMOURED.

88. INT. WEEKEND FESTIVAL FOYER. DAY.

A BOY *in Latin costume.*

BOY: [*to camera*] New steps . . .

Spinning headline shot: NEW STEPS RUMOURED.

89. INT. WEEKEND FESTIVAL FOYER. DAY.

An entire family dressed in ballroom costume.

FAMILY: [*in unison to camera*] New steps, new steps, new steps . . .

90. INT. BARRY FIFE'S OFFICE. DAY.

A Federation meeting out of control. The camera tracks slowly down the table towards BARRY FIFE. *Panicky Federation officials shout and argue amongst themselves. 'New steps', 'Pan Pacifics', 'my students', 'new steps', 'new steps' . . .* BARRY's *face, dark as a storm cloud, now fills the screen. He rises to speak.*

BARRY: There are no new steps.

> *A whirling headline shot fills the screen: FEDERATION PRESIDENT DENIES RUMOUR OF NEW STEPS.*

91. INT. BARRY'S BEDROOM. LATE NIGHT.

BARRY: I unequivocally state there are no new steps ratified for the Pan Pacific Grand Prix comprende?
> BARRY *and* CHARM *are in bed, naked except for a strategically draped sheet.*
[*slamming down the receiver*] This is getting out of hand.
> CHARM *moves beneath* BARRY.
Oh Charm, stop it. I'm trying to think – something's got to be done about this.

92. INT. KENDALL'S STUDIO. DOWNSTAIRS ROOM. DAY.

SHIRLEY, DOUG, CHARM, LES *and* BARRY *sit around a cheap laminex table.*

BARRY: . . . If you can't dance a step you can't teach it and

56

if you can't teach it – we might as well all pack up and go home. With young Liz available again you've got a chance to get your status quo vadis back, so to speak.

SHIRLEY: But Barry, we've tried everything we can to convince him.

BARRY: Except the truth.

> *There is an uncomfortable silence broken only by the sound of* DOUG *squirting Cedal breath freshener into his mouth.*

SHIRLEY: [*tentatively*] What do you mean?

BARRY: Look we all go back too far to beat around the bush I know we agreed that the past should be left in the past, but it's about time that lad learnt some home truths about where this kind of thing can lead.

> DOUG *noisily pushes his chair back and rises to his feet. He struggles to speak.*

DOUG: I'd better fill the drinks machine.

93. INT/EXT. TOLEDO MILK-BAR. BACK VERANDAH. DAY.

SCOTT, FRAN and RICO practice together. YA YA sashays to the record player and slips on a crackled version of a long forgotten Spanish pop tune. For a moment she flirts coquettishly with the group then all four explode into an impromptu and joyous routine. There is a flurry of rhythm as they finish together. SCOTT and FRAN gaze into each other's eyes, their lips almost touching. YA YA breaks the moment.

YA YA: You're ready kids, you're ready.

RICO: Yes, they're ready.

94. INT. KENDALL'S STUDIO. MAIN SALON. DAY.

The studio is empty. DOUG dances alone to the melancholy strains of a sentimental waltz. Though he moves with the same manic intensity, the standard of his dancing is unsettling. His soft, large eyes are streaming with tears.

SHIRLEY and BARRY's words echo ominously through the soundtrack.

SHIRLEY: We tried everything we can to convince him.
BARRY: Except the truth.

95. EXT. THE RIDGE. LATE AFTERNOON.

SCOTT and FRAN are silhouetted against a dark and brooding sunset.

SCOTT: Are you nervous about tomorrow?
FRAN: Yeah, are you?
SCOTT: I never thought we'd make it.
FRAN: [*smiles*] Me neither.
  Pause. A warm wind blows.
SCOTT: Fran . . . ?
FRAN: Yeah . . . ?
SCOTT: You know what I said about the rumba, and it being pretend?
FRAN: Yeah.
  SCOTT moves his face towards FRAN's.
SCOTT: Well . . .
FRAN: What . . . ?
SCOTT: I think I made a mistake . . .
  SCOTT leans toward FRAN and they kiss for the first time. They draw apart, staring into each other's eyes. SCOTT suddenly remembers.
  Oh no . . .
FRAN: What?
SCOTT: I promised Wayne I'd meet him and help him with his...
  FRAN looks into SCOTT's eyes.
FRAN and SCOTT: [*laughing*] Bogo Pogo!
FRAN: [*smiling*] Better not keep him waiting.
SCOTT: Vivir con miedo es como vivir a medias.
  FRAN leans forward and the couple passionately kiss.

59

96. INT. KENDALL'S STUDIO. MAIN SALON. LATE
AFTERNOON.

*The empty studio is flooded with afternoon light. SCOTT
enters and calls.*

SCOTT: Wayne! Wayne!
   *A large middle-aged man emerges from the kitchen. The
   bulky outline is familiar. The camera slams into an
   extreme close up of BARRY's smiling features. SCOTT is
   startled. He glances left and right sensing a trap.*
BARRY: [*amiably*] Wayne is not here. Hope you don't mind.
SCOTT: We know we can't win, but we're going to dance
   anyway, so let's not waste each other's time.
   SCOTT turns to go.
BARRY: He was the most beautiful dancer I'd ever seen.
SCOTT: [*stopping*] What?
   BARRY's eyes are moist.
BARRY: He could have been the greatest champion of them
   all; but he was like you. Threw it all away.
SCOTT: Who?
   *BARRY looks to the old black and white photograph on
   the wall.*
BARRY: The man in this photograph.
SCOTT: What are you talking about?
BARRY: [*shaking his head*] I'm talking about the man who
   was potentially the greatest ballroom dancer this
   country's ever seen. I'm talking about your father, Doug
   Hastings.
SCOTT: [*laughs*] Oh come on, Dad doesn't even dance.
   *BARRY cracks, his eyes fill with tears and we see a rare
   moment of true emotion from the man.*
BARRY: You think it's funny? You think it's funny do you? I
   worshipped that man, we all did. Doug Hastings was an
   inspiration to us all.
SCOTT: [*referring to the photo*] But that's Les. Les was
   Mum's partner.
BARRY: No, Scott, that's Doug. I know to look at him today

60

it's hard to believe, but once, once, ah once . . .

The photograph of SHIRLEY *and her partner animates to life. The couple skip through a saucy quick step. The dancers turn and we catch sight of the man's face. It is a young* DOUG HASTINGS.

Doug and Shirley Hastings were the best bloody couple this country had ever seen. Couple number 100. Y'know Scott, your Dad . . . he had it all, looks, charm, confidence. He had everything. Everything.

The young DOUG *roars.*

My God, he was magnificent. Samba, cha-cha, rumba, jive, anything, he could do anything! Brilliant. All the girls loved him . . .

DOUG *is dancing with four giggling, beehive coiffed girls.*

My goodness, he showed those chickies a thing or two.

Curtains open to reveal DOUG *joined in a routine by* BARRY. BARRY *and* DOUG *are joined by a young* LES. *They all dance.*

I was your Dad's best mate in those days, we used to scruff it together, y'know, swing it around. Lessie'd come along of course. The three of us together, the old gang. We were a bunch of old funsters.

Young SHIRLEY *emerges from behind a closed curtain.*

We all wanted to win of course, but with your Mum as your Dad's partner, we had no chance.

DOUG *and* SHIRLEY *are being presented with bouquets, trophies and ribbons.*

They were magnificent. They had it all before them. A perfect career and then everything changed. Your Dad became, I dunno, self-obsessed, focused on himself, a selfish dancer.

DOUG *and* SHIRLEY *dance.* DOUG *starts to improvise.*

I didn't know what to make of it. He started doing his own thing. Improvising. Throwing in crazy, wild, crowd-pleasing steps. A bit like yourself, Scott, Not always strictly ballroom.

DOUG *throws* SHIRLEY *up into the air, looks at his watch and shrugs.* SHIRLEY *flies through the air in panic.*

SHIRLEY falls into DOUG's arms.

Shirley'd put up with it for as long as she bloody-well could. It was only a matter of time before she eventually cracked.

SHIRLEY distraught as DOUG dances his own steps.

I tried to warn him. But no he wouldn't listen to any of us, he'd lost touch with reality. He was convinced he and your Mum could win the Pan Pacific Grand Prix dancing his own steps. Of course, they lost.

The curtains open to reveal young BARRY holding the winning trophy with young CHARM at his side.

I was lucky enough to win the title that year.

A screaming DOUG hurls a trophy into the studio mirror.

It was horrible. The shock sent Doug crazy. He vowed never to dance again.

DOUG sits forlornly with a rug over his knees staring into space.

For a while we didn't think he'd pull through. Slowly, little by little, day by day, he managed to crawl back from the dark pit of despair, and tack together some semblance of a life.

We return to the present. SCOTT is in the studio still holding the photograph.

When you were born, Doug found a reason to live. He vowed that one day you'd win the trophy that he could never win. That's why I've been so hard on you Scott. For Doug to see you so close and, go the same way he went, it would be too much for him to bear. I really think it'd kill him. I managed to save this as a souvenir. Doug got rid of everything else.

BARRY takes a pennant from his pocket.

Don't tell anyone I've got it.

SCOTT is shocked, barely able to speak. The pennant reads 'Doug and Shirley Hastings. State Champions 1967'.

SCOTT: Why didn't anyone tell me?

BARRY: Doug destroyed your mother's career. We had to keep it from you.

BARRY pauses. He fights back the tears as he struggles to contain his emotions.

Your father's proud Scott. He wouldn't want me to do this, but I'm begging you – dance with Liz and win the Pan Pacifics once, just once for Doug. He's suffered enough, Scott. Don't you think he deserves a little bit of happiness? [*He pauses and wipes the tears from his eyes.*] Ultimately it's up to you of course. You do what you think's best. [*He pats* SCOTT *on the shoulder and walks to the door, he turns.*] I know you'll make the right decision.

BARRY leaves. SCOTT *stands alone, shocked, unable to comprehend what he has just heard. He stares at the photograph, his mind in turmoil. Suddenly he turns and runs to the stairwell which leads to the downstairs room.*

97. INT. KENDALL'S STUDIO. DOUG'S ROOM. EVENING.

SCOTT *smashes open the downstairs cupboard and unleashes an avalanche of* DOUG's *memorabilia. Black and white photographs and spools of 8mm film spill onto the floor.* SCOTT *picks up a photo. It shows* SHIRLEY *with her tail-suited partner. We see his face – it is* DOUG. *As* SCOTT *unleashes a cry of anger and despair,* BARRY's *words echo in his head.*

BARRY: Dance with Liz, and win the Pan Pacifics once, just once for Doug. He's suffered enough Scott.

The lighting changes, an orchestra booms and SCOTT *is now suited in his tailcoat, spinning, spinning.* LIZ *joins him in her favourite yellow.*

98. INT. PAN PACIFIC GRAND PRIX. MAIN ARENA. NIGHT.

SCOTT *and* LIZ *are surrounded by hundreds of competitive dance couples. A kaleidoscope of colour in a huge indoor*

sports arena. This year's venue for the Pan Pacific Grand Prix.

J.J. SILVERS: Put your hands together ladies and gentlemen the magnificent, old-time Viennese. Thank you couples, you may leave the floor.

SCOTT and LIZ, arm-in-arm, walk from the floor. TINA leaves the floor in a huff followed by KEN who is slightly unsteady on his feet. SCOTT and LIZ are set upon by congratulatory members of the Kendall's studio.

SHIRLEY: [*handing SCOTT cordial in a plastic cup*] Very good darling, very good indeed.

LIZ: Thank you.

SHIRLEY: Very good.

LES: Straight down the line, couldn't fault it.

VANESSA: Thanks, Mrs Hastings.

LIZ glances across the floor to where KEN, again with his thermos, gestures expansively to well-wishers in the crowd.

TINA: Jesus, Ken.

KEN: I only had one drink.

LIZ: Poor Tina. It's like dancing in a brewery.

As SCOTT wipes the perspiration from his brow, he looks towards his father but DOUG stares away refusing to acknowledge him.

J.J. SILVERS: Couples for the All Girls Beginners' Final, please take the floor.

KYLIE: Look Scott, it's Fran.

SCOTT turns to see FRAN and NATALIE take the floor for the Beginners' Final. FRAN holds her head high, proud and defiant.

VANESSA: I didn't think she'd turn up.

LIZ: [*under her breath*] Back in beginners where she belongs.

CLARRY: And she stole my partner.

WAYNE: You made the right decision, mate.

SCOTT ignores him, drawn by FRAN. LES takes SCOTT by the shoulders and eases his attention away from the floor. The other studio members huddle in to listen as he addresses SCOTT.

LES: I know at times it's been confusing for you, Scott, but I'm speaking for the whole studio, when I say that by putting your trust in the Federation you've done the right thing, and I think you'll find this reflected in the results of the big one yet to come, the open Latin final.

LES's speech is supported by a 'here, here'. But SCOTT's *attention is drawn to the unnerving sight of* DOUG *filming* FRAN *with his Super 8. One by one, the Kendalls turn to observe* DOUG's *activity. When he has captured their attention, he turns to* SCOTT.

DOUG: Son, can I bend your ear for a tick . . . ?

SHIRLEY in an agitated state, shoves a suit-bag at SCOTT.

SHIRLEY: Doug, don't be stupid. He's got to get ready for the Latin.

LES: I'd better get back to the Scrutineers' table.

LIZ grabs SCOTT's *arm.*

LIZ: Come on Scott

LES: [*giving him an encouraging pat*] Go for it boy.

SCOTT makes his way through the crowd, his eyes fixed on FRAN *who is completing her routine with* NATALIE.

99. INT. PAN PACIFIC GRAND PRIX. MAIN ARENA. NIGHT.

YA YA and RICO *watch as* FRAN *completes her routine.*

YA YA: Está preciosa. [*She looks beautiful.*]

RICO: Si encuentro a ese cabrón, lo mato. [*If I find that little bastard, I'll kill him.*]

100. INT. PAN PACIFIC GRAND PRIX. TRANSIT TUNNEL. NIGHT.

SCOTT stops at the changing-room door. He slowly turns and looks through the door that opens out on to the main arena. He can see FRAN dancing the gipsy tap. He suddenly turns and darts back into the transit tunnel.

101. INT. PAN PACIFIC. GRAND PRIX. TRANSIT TUNNEL. NIGHT.

WAYNE and VANESSA practice the Bogo Pogo step intensely in the transit tunnel.

VANESSA: It isn't, Wayne. It's quick three and two and two three.

> *WAYNE, not convinced, takes VANESSA through the step again.*

WAYNE: You go back to the ballpoint from there.

> *BARRY FIFE passes the desperately practising couple.*

Excuse me Mr Fife.

> *BARRY is disturbed to be accosted by a mere peasant.*

BARRY: Ah . . . what is it son?

WAYNE: It's the Bogo Pogo, Mr Fife, you know that step you suggested.

BARRY: Did I? . . .

WAYNE: Yeah, you said you'd show us if I arranged that other thing for you, remember?

BARRY: Bit of a hurry at the moment, son.

WAYNE: You know my partner, Vanessa Cronin.

> *BARRY takes in VANESSA's voluptuousness.*

BARRY: Well hello sweetie. Having a bit of trouble with the old bogo pogo are we?

> *Seizing the opportunity to impress, BARRY takes VANESSA in dance position, pressing his body against her.*

The trick to that is to go down on one heel ball. Then pull the weight up onto the chest, puffing it out proud like a peacock!

> *BARRY demonstrates, writhing with VANESSA in the syncopated step.*

Then syncopating a quick two and three and three and four. Comprende?

> *BARRY departners VANESSA.*

WAYNE: Gee, thanks Mr Fife.

BARRY: Got to run kids, good luck for today.

102. INT. PAN PACIFIC GRAND PRIX. TRANSIT TUNNEL. NIGHT.

SCOTT runs through the crowded transit tunnel, he collides with DOUG.

DOUG: Can I bend –
SCOTT: Not now Dad.

103. INT. PAN PACIFIC GRAND PRIX. DARK TUNNEL. NIGHT.

SCOTT has arrived at the place FRAN was, but she is gone, successful in her attempt to avoid him. He turns to go. We see FRAN's startled face as they accidentally collide. A moment of stillness between the two.

FRAN: What happened to a life lived in fear and all that stuff?
SCOTT: Fran . . .
FRAN: You really are a gutless wonder.
> *FRAN turns defiantly and walks away, refusing to hear SCOTT.*
SCOTT: [*pursuing her*] There's a reason for this.
FRAN: I don't want to hear.
SCOTT: Listen to me.
FRAN: No.
SCOTT: It's hard for me too, Fran.
FRAN: Hard? [*She spits the word at him*] Hard? How hard do you think it's been for me? To get you to dance with me in the first place – Frangipannidelasqueegymop. Wash the coffee cups Fran. How's your skin Fran? Hard?!
SCOTT: You don't understand.
FRAN: I understand, you've got your Pan Pacifics to win and I'm back in beginners where I belong.
> *FRAN turns and pushes her way through the crowd.*
SCOTT: Fran!
> *As SCOTT pursues her suddenly DOUG pops up like a jack-in-the-box.*

69

DOUG: Son can I bend your ear for a tick?
SCOTT: Not now.
    FRAN disappears into the crowd.
DOUG: [*uncharacteristically strong*] Yes, now Scott.

104. INT. PAN PACIFIC. GRAND PRIX. SEATS. MAIN ARENA. NIGHT.

J.J. SILVERS: And now, ladies and gentlemen, the main event of the evening, the one we've all been waiting for the Pan Pacific Grand Prix Amateur Five Dance Latin Final.

105. INT. PAN PACIFIC GRAND PRIX. STAIRS. NIGHT.

WAYNE and VANESSA pursue BARRY FIFE through the crowd. He disappears around a corner.

WAYNE: . . . but you ball changed on the one.
VANESSA: It doesn't matter, Wayne.
WAYNE: Come on!

106. INT. PAN PACIFIC GRAND PRIX. BACK STAGE. NIGHT.

SCOTT: It's okay Dad, I'm dancing with Liz.
DOUG: But there's something you must know, something about the past.
SCOTT: Don't worry Dad, I know . . .

107. INT. PAN PACIFIC GRAND PRIX. BACKSTAGE. NIGHT.

VANESSA and WAYNE pursue BARRY.

WAYNE: Mr Fife.
VANESSA: Wayne . . .
    As they round the corner, they catch sight of the disturbing spectacle of KEN. His eyes are bloodshot, his make-up is streaked with sweat, his speech is slurred

and he is obviously losing it. BARRY *shakes him as* TINA *looks on, disturbed.*

BARRY: I've set it up for you to win, no matter how you dance.

KEN: I can't go out there. I've lost the old magic.

BARRY: [*a hoarse whisper*] Pull yourself together Railings!

108. INT. PAN PACIFIC GRAND PRIX. BACK STAGE. NIGHT.

DOUG: But you don't understand, I've always regretted . . .

SCOTT: [*exasperated*] . . . dancing your own steps at the Pan Pacific Grand Prix I know, I'm not going to make that same mistake.

DOUG: I never danced at the Pan Pacific Grand Prix.

SCOTT: Barry told me you lost the Pan Pacific Grand Prix dancing your own steps.

DOUG: Barry! . . .

109. INT. PAN PACIFIC GRAND PRIX. BACKSTAGE AREA. NIGHT.

From WAYNE *and* VANESSA's *concealed point of view we see* KEN *sweating and shaking as* BARRY *desperately tries to communicate.*

BARRY: Your year, Ken. Just get on the floor, go through the motions and it's in the bag. [*With a chilling intensity*] When Hastings loses, his credibility will be shot. I'll just go and polish the trophy.

TINA: Thanks Mr Fife.

110. INT. PAN PACIFIC GRAND PRIX. BACKSTAGE. NIGHT.

DOUG: Barry was the one who convinced her . . .

SCOTT: Convinced who?

J.J. SILVERS: Couple No. 100, Scott Hastings and Elizabeth Holt.

DOUG: Your mother.

SHIRLEY arrives on the scene, charging like a bull. She grabs SCOTT, dragging him towards the panicking LIZ, who waits to take the floor.

SHIRLEY: Doug, he's being called you silly man!

111. INT. PAN PACIFIC GRAND PRIX. BACKSTAGE. NIGHT.

VANESSA tries to restrain WAYNE as he makes his way toward the side of the stage.

J.J. SILVERS: Wayne Burns and Vanessa Cronin. Couple number 176, Jonathon Drench and Emily Waters.

VANESSA: Wayne, we're being called. It's none of our business.

WAYNE beckons to LES at the Scrutineers' table.

WAYNE: Les! Les!

VANESSA hands WAYNE her earring.

VANESSA: Here use this.

WAYNE throws it, attracting LES's attention.

J.J. SILVERS: This is the final call for couple number 54, Wayne Burns and Vanessa Cronin.

112. INT. PAN PACIFIC GRAND PRIX. BACKSTAGE NIGHT.

TINA and KEN hurry past the now frantic LIZ and take the floor.

J.J. SILVERS: Couple No. 69. Ken Railings and Tina Sparkle!

SCOTT: What are you talking about Dad?

DOUG: I never danced at the Pan Pacific Grand Prix.

SHIRLEY: Shut up Doug . . . !

DOUG: Barry convinced your mother to dance with Les instead of me at the Pan Pacifics.

SHIRLEY: Stop it.

SCOTT: What?

SHIRLEY: Don't listen to him Scott, it's got nothing to do with this.

SCOTT: Why didn't you dance with Dad?

SHIRLEY: He wanted to dance his silly steps. We would have lost.

DOUG: You lost anyway, Shirley. You should have stuck by me for better or for worse.

SHIRLEY: I did it for you Doug .

DOUG: It cost us our dream, Shirley.

SHIRLEY is starting to cry.

SHIRLEY: Barry convinced me . . . There was too much at stake. Our dancing career was on the line. I couldn't throw that all away on a dream. We had to survive. We would never have been able to teach.

The curtains open.

J.J. SILVERS: One hundred, Scott Hastings and Elizabeth Holt.

LIZ: [*screaming*] Scott!

SHIRLEY: Don't listen to him Scott. Get on that floor. You can win Scott, win, win.

DOUG: Son, it was the dancing that mattered.

SHIRLEY: He doesn't know what he's talking about. It's your day, your day. Get out there and dance.

DOUG: We should have put it above everything else. We had the chance, but we were scared. We walked away. [*turning to SCOTT*] We've lived our lives in fear.

SCOTT stops in his tracks. The words resonate in his head. The orchestra heralds the paso doble. In slow motion SCOTT looks to LIZ, he sees her hand outstretched, her lips silently imploring him to dance. His mother, her face anguished. Then suddenly to the urgent rhythm of the paso, he turns on his heels and is off. LIZ's face explodes into tears.

SHIRLEY: No, Scott, No!

On the dance floor couples burst into their opening routines, striving to be noticed.

113. INT. PAN PACIFIC GRAND PRIX. DARK TUNNEL. NIGHT.

SCOTT is searching desperately through the crowd.

114. INT. PAN PACIFIC GRAND PRIX. MAIN ARENA. NIGHT.

KEN and TINA shine on the dance floor.

115. INT. PAN PACIFIC. GRAND PRIX. SCRUTINEERS' TABLE. NIGHT.

BARRY, at the Scrutineers' table, has his eyes glued to KEN as he leans discreetly towards CHARM.

BARRY: [*under his breath*] Break out the Bollinger, sweet chops.

116. INT. PAN PACIFIC GRAND PRIX. BACKSTAGE. NIGHT.

A close-up of LES's disbelieving face.

LES: Are you sure?
    WAYNE and VANESSA nod.
WAYNE: We heard them.

117. INT. PAN PACIFIC GRAND PRIX. TUNNEL. NIGHT.

SCOTT bursts from the dance centre just as FRAN, RICO and YA YA are about to leave.

SCOTT: Fran!
    FRAN turns.
FRAN: Why aren't you . . .
SCOTT: There's no time. Do you still want to dance with me?
    FRAN considers. For a moment time stands still. Then

76

slowly she nods and smiles. YA YA *magically produces the dress.*
YA YA: I brought this just in case.
SCOTT: Come on!
RICO: Olé!
   They race to the floor.

118. INT. PAN PACIFIC GRAND PRIX. SCRUTINEER'S TABLE. NIGHT.

The competition rages as LES *taps* BARRY *vigorously on the shoulder.*

LES: I want a word with you.
BARRY: Pull yourself together. It's not my fault the boy chickened out.
LES: It wouldn't have made any difference anyway.
BARRY: Out the back.

119. INT. PAN PACIFIC GRAND PRIX BACKSTAGE. NIGHT.

LES *and* BARRY *argue behind the backstage curtain.*

LES: I know what's going on. It doesn't matter what Scott dances out there today.
BARRY: You betrayed his father, what do you expect?
LES: But Doug wanted me to dance with Shirley – you told me that.
BARRY: Yeah, but it's easy to believe what you want to hear, isn't it Les?
LES: [*white with rage*] You won't get away with this.
   BARRY *pokes* LES *in the chest.*
BARRY: Listen, you pathetic fag, you hear that? That is the future of dance sport and no-one, but no-one is going to change that.
   With this the music heralds the cavalry. BARRY *draws back the curtain. Suddenly like a shooting star,* SCOTT *slides on his knees nearly the whole length of the floor.*

He stops at a pair of ruby red shoes framed by layers of Spanish tulle.

J.J. SILVERS: What the . . . ?

SCOTT and FRAN begin to tell their story. What we see is truly great dance. Time stands still as each kick and snap resounds throughout the audience – the crowd reacting as if at a bullfight. LES is mute with shock and pride. BARRY after recoiling, moves onto the stage and pulls the microphone from J.J. SILVERS.

BARRY: Give me that bloody thing!

He lifts it to his lips. Suddenly WAYNE appears running hard. Launching himself through space he dives the full length of the stage and wrenches the microphone cord from the socket.

WAYNE: No you don't!

BARRY: Cut the music!

KYLIE's and LUKE's faces pop up over the edge of the stage.

KYLIE: He's going to cut the music.

They scamper across the stage towards the record booth. BARRY moves towards the record booth.

LES: Barry?

WHACK – A beautiful right hook. BARRY goes down.

KYLIE: . . . get inside the room

LUKE slips into the booth and locks the door. SCOTT and FRAN's passionate and daring paso doble has electrified the auditorium. LES is kneeling on the stage profoundly weeping. YA YA and RICO are in the crowd, they beam with pride. KYLIE and LUKE are in the record booth. They cheer.

120. INT. PAN PACIFIC GRAND PRIX. BACKSTAGE. NIGHT.

We discover CHARM LEACHMAN backstage. She glances furtively left and right before yanking the record booth's power cord from its wall socket.

121. INT. PAN PACIFIC GRAND PRIX. MAIN ARENA. NIGHT

Suddenly – catastrophe, the music is silenced. The dancers stop in their tracks, halted mid-routine. Pandemonium fills the auditorium as heads turn, searching for the source of the interruption. BARRY seizes the moment, he stands and re-plugs the microphone.

122. INT. PAN PACIFIC GRAND PRIX. RECORD BOOTH. NIGHT.

LUKE desperately pushes buttons and twiddles dials on the sound console.

LUKE: It's not working.

123. INT. PAN PACIFIC GRAND PRIX. STAGE. NIGHT.

BARRY almost shouts into the microphone.

BARRY: We have a DISQUALIFICATION – this is Barry Fife speaking. Scott Hastings and partner are suspended until further notice.
  During this alarming announcement the crowd fall silent.
Will Scott Hastings and partner please leave the floor.
  SCOTT and FRAN hold their position.
This is a final warning for Scott Hastings and partner to leave the floor.
  From the crowd there is no support, just a taut unfriendly silence. Slowly SCOTT looks to FRAN – they turn to leave the floor. Suddenly a single loud, hard, clap shatters the stillness. Then another, and another, slow, even and strong. The crowd desperately search, unclear where it comes from. BARRY's eyes are unsettled. The clapping becomes louder and louder. The camera tracks past SCOTT and FRAN, through the parting crowd to find the source of the disturbance, it is . . .

DOUG. *He clashes his hands together in strong defiant beats. As he claps, he walks towards the floor. He seems to grow in height with every step but still there is no support from the audience, until . . .* YA YA *begins to beat a counter-rhythm. Then* RICO *joins.*

YA YA: Listen to the rhythm, don't be scared.

LES *rises from the floor and joins* DOUG's *beating.* NATALIE *joins the rhythm.* WAYNE *and* VANESSA *follow. Now* CLARRY *and even* LIZ *join the clapping. Others follow, now, more and more people, building to the world's largest percussive orchestra.* SCOTT *looks to* FRAN. *They know that rhythm – without music, and to the pure power of human rhythm,* SCOTT *and* FRAN *begin to dance.*

124. INT. PAN PACIFIC GRAND PRIX. BACKSTAGE.NIGHT.

Backstage. KYLIE *confronts* CHARM, *who sheepishly guards the disconnected power cord.*

CHARM: No you don't, little miss.

KYLIE: [*shaking her head*] Shame on you Mrs Leachman . . .

KYLIE *reaches for the cord, but* CHARM *pulls her away. as* CHARM *grapples with* KYLIE *she looks up just in time to see* LIZ *push the power chord firmley back into it's socket.* LIZ *stares defiantly at* CHARM.

125. INT. PAN PACIFIC GRAND PRIX. MAIN ARENA. NIGHT.

Music swells back into the auditorium and the finale of SCOTT *and* FRAN's *paso doble is accompanied by both the crowd and the majestic closing bars of 'Cane Espana'. A powerful final chord then mayhem. The response is unearthly.* BARRY *is horrified. He moves back from the thunderous defiant applause only to connect with the trophy table, bringing it down upon himself.*

126. INT. PAN PACIFIC GRAND PRIX. MAIN ARENA. NIGHT.

DOUG slowly walks through the crowd. He stops in front of SHIRLEY, looks her in the eye and asks the question she has waited twenty-five years to hear.

DOUG: **Shall we dance?**

> *SHIRLEY hesitates, tears streaming from her eyes. She meets DOUG's gaze and they take the floor to the cheers of the crowd. Now WAYNE and VANESSA, CLARRY and NATALIE. Now THREE more couples. FIVE more. TEN. KYLIE and LUKE dance SCOTT's samba. YA YA dances with LES. The floor is flooded in a sea of celebration. As the samba finishes, we hear the final bars of the 'Blue Danube' and the red velvet curtain rings down.*

THE END

FILM CREDITS

Screenplay by Baz Luhrmann and Craig Pearce from a screenplay by Baz Luhrmann and Andrew Bovell, from an original idea by Baz Luhrmann. Based on the N.I.D.A. stage production, devised and developed by the original cast: Glenn Keenan, Baz Luhrmann, Catherine McClements, Helen Mutkins, Tony Poli, Jamie Robertson, Nell Schofield, Sonia Todd. And further developed by the Six Years Old Company: Tyler Coppin, Di Emery, Lisa Kelly, Glenn Keenan, Baz Luhrmann, Genevieve Mooy, Tara Morice, Mark Owen-Taylor, Craig Pearce.

Sound Recordist, Ben Osmo/First Assistant Director, Keith Heygate/Production Manager, Fiona McConaghy/Casting, Faith Martin/Production Co-ordinator, Rowena Talacko/Production Secretary, Christine Gordon/Producer's Secretary, Trish Cameron/Extras Casting, Faith Martin/Production Assistant/Runner Amanda Higgs/Locations, Lisa Hennessey/Unit Manager, Justin Plummer/Production Accountant, Michele D'Arcey/Second Assistant Director, P.J. Voeten/Third Assistant Director, John Martin/Nurse/Assistant Director, Sue Andrews/Continuity, Jo Weeks/Focus Puller, John Platt/Clapper Loader, Leah Ashenhurst/Steadicam Operators, Ian Jones, David Woodward/Second Camera Operators, Ross Berryman, Andrew McLean/Boom Operator, Andy Duncan/Playback Operator, Jack Friedman/Sound Dept. Attachment, Stuart Cottom/Gaffer, Reg Garside/Best Boy, Gary Hill/Electrics, Alan Dunstan/Casual Electric, Steve Gray/Key Grip, Paul Thompson/Assistant Grip, Alan Hansen/Art Director, Martin Brown/Props Buyers/Set Dressers, Martin Brown, Bill Marron, Rebecca Cohen, Justine Thompson/Art Dept. Co-ordinator, Julieanne Mills/Standby Props, George Zammit/Art Dept. Runner, Tony Campbell/Art Dept. Attachment, Elizabeth Mary Moore/Draughtsmen/Model Makers, Michael Philips, Duncan Stemler/Construction, Rob Ricketson Design Pty, Terry Mathews, Mary Baumont, Radar Pty Limited, Peter Grady/Vehicle Rig, Jonathan Clouston/Scenic Artists, Steve Smith, Alan Craft, East Coast Signs Pty Limited, Lynn Rowland/Wardrobe Supervisor, Peter Bevan/Wardrobe Assistant, Kym Barrett/Standby Wardrobe, Lyn Askew/Costumiers, Nola Lowe, Anthony Phillips, Christopher Essex/Street Costumes, Catherine Martin/Costume Detailing, Suzette Waters, Kym Bywater, Melissa Harrison/Make-up Designer, Lesley Vanderwalt/Hair Designer, Paul Williams/Make-up and Hair Assistant, Rebecca Simons/Assistant Choreographer & Ballroom Tutor, Ray Mather/Ballroom Advisor, Sonia Kruger/Additional Choreography, Paul Mercurio/Flamenco Dance Tutor, Antonio Vargas/Liz Holt double, Tania McGuinness/First Assistant Picture Editor, Jane Moran/Second Assistant Picture Editor, Nick Cole/Mixed by, Roger Savage, Ian McLoughlin, Phil Judd/Mixed at Soundfirm/Effects Editors, Wayne Pashley, Julius Chan/Dialogue Editor, Antony Gray/Assistant Editor, David Grusovin/Foley Artist, Gerry Long/Foley Recording, Steve Burgess, Paul Pirola/Sound

STRICTLY BALLROOM

Effects mixed by Bruce Brown/Assistant Engineer, Simon B. Sheridan/Recording & Post Production Studios, Albert Studios/Sound Tools Editing, Michael Costa/Additional Orchestration, Ric Formosa/Concertmaster, Phillip Hartl/Choral Voices, Sydney Philharmonia Choir/Copyright Clearance, Nicole Sheridan/Stills Photographer, Philip Le Masurier/Unit Publicist, Dina Gillespie/Safety Officer, Claude Lambert/Caterer, John Faithfull/Unit Driver, Jeremy Hutchinson/Final Championships filmed at Melbourne Sports & Entertainment Centre/Laboratory, Atlab Australia/Opticals, Roger Cowland/Grading, Arthur Cambridge/Laboratory Liaison, Ian Russell/Titles Design, Bill Marron & Catherine Martin/Animation, Bill Marron & John Skibinski/Titles Shoot, The Funny Farm/Camera Equipment, Samuelson Film Service/Insurance Brokers, Hammond Jewell Pty Ltd/Auditor, Rosenfeld, Kant & Co/Legal Advisors, Michael Frankel & Co. Solicitors/Completion Guarantor, First Australian Completion Bond Company Pty Ltd.

Special thanks to the Albert Family, J. Albert & Son Pty Ltd, The Australian Opera, Six Years Old Company, Sydney Theatre Company, Sydney Dance Company, National Institute of Dramatic Art, Ronin Films, Burrows Limited, Kirsty Albert, Keith Bain, Dennis Dove, Trevor Farrant, Ross & Barbi Fludder, Mark Hartley, Margaret Lonsdale, Barry Lowe, Neville Lowe, Mandy Luhrmann, Maureen McCabe, Ray McMahon, Juan & Carmen Dos Maravillas, Lynn-Maree Milburn, Barry Mole, Robert Murphy, Doug & Sue Potter, Gordon Scholls, Barry & Shirley Wall, Juan Carlos Walshe, Katie Wright. Baz Luhrmann acknowledges the special contribution of Catherine Martin and Bill Marron in the development of this film.